TASTE

By the Author

Jolt

Whirlwind Romance

Just Say Yes: The Proposal

Taste

TASTE

by

Kris Bryant

2016

TASTE

ISBN 13: 978-1-62639-718-7

This Trade Paperback Original Is Published By
Bold Strokes Books, Inc.
P.O. Box 249
Valley Falls, NY 12185

First Edition: October 2016

Credits
Editor: Ashley Tillman
Production Design: Susan Ramundo
Cover Design By Sheri (graphicartist2020@hotmail.com)

Acknowledgments

My writing family grows with every book. I've made incredible connections with so many women in this industry, not to mention the readers who make our success possible. Thank you, Rad & Sandy, who still publish me even though I am rather difficult. Ashley pushes me hard to make me the best writer I can be and I am forever grateful for her as my editor. A sincere thank you to my betas Cindy and Nadine who helped me keep this book in line. I would need a separate book to thank all of my friends, new and old, who help me along this fantastic journey. Just know who you are and know that yes, I mean you. Here's to 48 seconds. Here's to late night snacks and early morning donuts.

Here's to a life full of love, passion, and taste.

Dedication

To Deb who gave me the idea because I'm always
stealing the remote to watch cooking shows.

CHAPTER ONE

"Turn!" I yell at the car in front of me. I'm already seven minutes late and the person in front of me, who obviously isn't in the same kind of hurry I am, is killing my patience. I hate being late. I lean back in my car and slowly count to ten to calm down. My clock flips and now I'm eight minutes late. I can see Kirkwood Culinary Academy up ahead. I'm twenty-seven years old and I still get butterflies on the first day of school. Technically, it's the first day of my last semester at the academy where I will finally complete my culinary apprenticeship and become a certified chef. When I quit law school and told my family, my mother sank down on the couch and sobbed. She handled my coming out ten years ago much better. I know she wants what's best for me, but in her mind, what's best equals money. In my mind, and in my heart, it's happiness. Cooking is my true talent. I have a relationship with food that I treat with respect. Food talks to me. I talk back. Unfortunately, I can't get to class because not everybody is in a hurry. I say a quick "thank you" to whoever is listening when the old man finally turns. I whip across traffic directly on his tail. The second I can pass him, I do. I skid into the parking lot and grab the closest spot I can find. I choke on my seat belt before remembering to unlatch it. Karma for being an impatient ass to the little old man. I sprint to the heavy doors and barge through them, ignoring the startled students lounging in the chairs by the entrance.

I find my class and quietly close the door, hoping to slip into an empty chair in the back of the class. No such luck. There are only two seats open. One is easy to get to, but in the front row. The other is in the third row, but I'd have to climb over students to reach it. Since I'm positive I've already irritated the new teacher, I decide to take the seat near her and not disrupt class further. She looks up from her quick review of the syllabus and we make eye contact. If we were at a bar, a grocery store, anywhere but here, I would give her a flirtatious smile. She's absolutely gorgeous. I stand there for a moment or two before she lifts her eyebrow at me.

"Chef, I'm sorry for being late. It won't happen again." I quickly drop into the open seat, breaking eye contact only to make sure my ass lands in the chair and not on the floor.

"I'm sure it won't." Her voice is low and dark; the huskiness sends chills across my body. This class just got more interesting. I grab a pen as she hands me a copy of the syllabus. Her name is Taryn Ellis. "This is probably the only day we will be sitting. The rest of the time will be spent in the kitchen. Are there any questions so far?"

Um, yes. Who are you? Where did you come from? Are you single? "I know you're new to the academy. What made you want to come here and teach?" I ask. I know all of the instructors here because I've worked closely with each one over the years. She looks at me in surprise. "I'm sorry if you've already answered that."

"No, it's a good question. I was asked by the Academy to come and teach. Their schedule fit mine, so I said yes."

"Are you from another institution or restaurant?" I hear a few students snicker. "I'm not trying to be rude, I'm just curious." I don't want Taryn to think I'm somehow making fun of her.

"Both, actually. I worked as Executive Chef at Rally's downtown for a year and the Culinary Institution here in town." Before I have a chance to ask her any more questions, she resumes the conversation about class expectations and goals for the students. I find her fascinating. She's beautiful, probably in her early thirties, and has an accent. I can't tell if it's British or Australian.

She brings up the three students still eligible for the Excellence in Culinary Arts Scholarship to attend another culinary school for ten months in Venice, Italy. My competition is fierce. Scott McDonnell is a few years older than I am, and we have battled the last two and a half years. Mary Martin is a distant third, but her pastries kick ass and she has beaten us both with desserts. When Taryn calls my name and realizes I'm the third, she has a hard time hiding her surprise.

"Well, Miss Katherine Blake, hopefully your cooking is better than your timing," she says. She's smiling this time so I know she's teasing.

"Ki. Call me Ki."

"Quit flirting, Ki," Scott says. He pokes my back with his pen. I try not to cringe and do my best to hold eye contact with Taryn. She pretends not to hear him and I pretend not to be embarrassed.

"Over the last few years, you've grown as chefs, learned how to run a restaurant, and how to plate. Our goal is to fine tune all of what you've learned, improve your palates, and learn how to cook under pressure. Even though everybody here interns at their choice of restaurant or food service as part of the program, I'm going to throw you into different environments and see how well you perform. There will be a few nights we will have class, but I will let you know well in advance so you can make the appropriate arrangements." A few students shuffle at their desks, obviously not happy, but nobody says anything. At least not on the first day.

"Well, if there are no more questions, let's get cooking." She glances at the clock. "I'm giving you the afternoon to prepare me a dish of your choosing. It can be any style of cooking. If you can find it in the kitchen, you can cook it. I want to be able to gauge where you are myself. Today, we start fresh. No looking at recipes or pulling up something on your phones or laptops. Let's see how well you do from memory."

She dismisses us with a quick wave of her hand and we scurry for prime spots in the kitchen. I feel like I'm in an episode of *Top Chef.* I find a spot near the refrigerators, but far enough away so that I'm not bothered by people running back and forth to get ingredients. I take a deep breath, close my eyes and think. What would a woman who lives to cook, loves to cook, wants to teach others to cook, want to taste right now? She's slender so I'm guessing she doesn't indulge much in the classic French cooking style where everything is drowned in butter, or bathed in heavy cream. No, she likes to eat healthy. I decide on cedar smoked salmon with rosemary mustard. When I open my eyes, I find her looking at me before she looks down at her laptop. I don't know why, but the look she gives me fills me with hope. I feel encouraged. I don't see her look at Scott, or Mary, or any of the other students in the class. I'm even more determined to impress her.

Cooking has always calmed me. Regardless of time constraints. When I'm in the zone, nothing bothers me. The only time I'm arrogant is in the kitchen.

"Chefs, don't forget hats and coats," she says. Shit. In my haste this afternoon, I forgot mine. Strike two. I slink over to her.

"Chef, I forgot mine. May I borrow a set?" She looks up at me.

"Bad day, Miss Blake?" she asks.

"You have no idea, Chef," I say. Charlie, a regular at the diner I work at, had a heart attack right there in the restaurant. I didn't have time to go back to my apartment to grab my things. I was happy to make it to class at all. She unlocks the supply cabinet and hands me a hat and a clean jacket.

"Thank you so much," I say. "This won't happen again." She gives me a look. "Really," I add. I head back to my station. I have a lot of ground to cover in a short amount of time.

I watch as she brings the fork up to her mouth. A nice mouth with straight, white teeth, and full red lips worthy of tasting perfection. Just watching her is such a turn on. I have an incredible urge to feed her, and I can't help but stare at her mouth as she tastes my food. For the briefest of moments, she closes her eyes. When she turns to face me the look in her eyes is that of pure gratification. I know I nailed it.

"Very good, Chef," she says. She places the fork on the plate and I notice her hand is slightly shaking. I don't know if my nearness is affecting her or if it's my food. Either way, I'm suppressing the biggest girl squeal of my life right now. I respectfully nod at her and head back to my work station. I wink at Scott as I walk by and he scowls at me. I smile, remembering how she told him his lamb shanks were undercooked. He really is a good chef, but he's too competitive and rushes. Hopefully, his impatience helps me win the scholarship this final semester.

I clean my station and wait for the rest of the students to finish. I'm dragging, hoping for some alone time with Taryn. Not just because I want praise for my cooking, but because I really want to get to know her. Scrubbing the work station again just makes me look stupid. I decide to grab my bag and head out. Tomorrow is a new day. Our eyes meet when I head out the door.

"I won't be late tomorrow," I say.

She smiles. "I know."

"And I'll remember my jacket and hat."

"I know."

CHAPTER TWO

H as anybody heard how Charlie's doing?" I ask anybody who can hear me as I walk through the kitchen doors of Bud's Diner. Ashley is the only one close by.

"He's hanging in there," she says. I exhale quietly. We've had some crazy things happen in the diner. Yesterday made the top five list along with a drive-by shooting, a drug bust, a fire in the kitchen, and when one of our waitresses went into early labor. I love the diner. There is so much character here. It's been my favorite place to intern so far. I'm learning how to cook rich and delicious southern and soul food, and they are learning how to incorporate some of the classic French cooking I've shown them into what they already know.

This job has my mother crying. She expects me to at least work at the finest restaurant in town, but I tell her I have to learn it all in order to do my job to the best of my ability. If I win the scholarship to Italy, I might redeem myself a bit with her.

"That was scary," I say. It really was. I'm a complete mess in situations of extreme stress unless there is food preparation involved. The only thing I was good for yesterday was holding Charlie's hand. The five minutes it took for the ambulance to arrive was the longest five minutes of my life. "So what's the special for today?"

"Ham hocks and beans," Ashley says. I nod my approval. Perfect for this time of year. Warm, stick-to-your-ribs comfort food.

"I'll make my cornbread." I grab two cast iron skillets and throw them into the oven to heat up. I whip up the ingredients along with a dash of cinnamon and honey to give it more sweetness and flavor.

"How was your first day?" Bud asks. He does most of the cooking around here. I work in the mornings and I help get lunch started.

"Well, to start things off, I was late to class. Then I forgot my jacket and my hat and had to borrow from the new teacher, who, by the way, is gorgeous. We had to cook her anything we wanted."

"Did you wow her?" he asks.

I smile at him. "I think so. She said 'very good, chef' and she closed her eyes when she took a bite." I sigh remembering her mouth and how her brown eyes lit up.

"And that's just day one. You have so many other dishes to show her before this semester ends. How did the others do?"

"Ha! She told Scott his lamb was undercooked and was too salty, but praised Mary for her strawberry shortcake. I'm not worried about her though."

"Maybe we should be working on desserts with you. How about sweet potato pie, or pecan pie?"

"I know how to make those desserts," I say. Not very well, though, and we both know it.

"Does your teacher like desserts?" he asks.

"Mary was the only one who made anything sweet, so I'm sure it was a treat."

"How about strawberry-rhubarb pie?" That perks my interest. I can never seem to get the pie to firm up just right, no matter how much cornstarch I use.

"Perfect. Today?"

"This week sometime. We have quite a few things to get done today and tomorrow unless you want to come in tonight," he says. My cat, Sophia, is ready to disown me. I'm sure I will pay for it tonight when she prances and dances across my body while I'm trying to sleep. I've been spending several extra nights at the diner this week trying to perfect fried chicken. Bud doesn't mind as long as I clean up after myself. Plus, whatever we don't eat or sell, Bud donates to his church's food kitchen.

"Thanks, but I think I need to stay home tonight and relax. Also, Sophia is getting pissed that I'm not home more," I say.

Bud laughs. "My wife's the same way. It's a good thing you don't have one of those," he says. I shrug. I think it would be kind of cool to share my life with somebody. My past girlfriends have all been younger, carefree, and emotionally unavailable. I'm ready for the grown up kind of romance.

We cook in companionable silence. We both prepare the breakfast orders as they come up. In the meantime, Bud thickens his ham and beans, and I take the cornbread out and slice it into equal portions. The heat lamp will keep them warm until orders come in. The breakfast crowd shuffles out and within thirty minutes, the lunch crowd files in and orders are up. I enjoy plating the food as much as I enjoy cooking. Bud thinks I try too hard. I tell him I make art in thirty seconds or less.

CHAPTER THREE

L et's go around the room and find out what everybody cooked since the last time we saw one another," Taryn says. We are standing around the center cooking station before she starts a demonstration on the proper way to prepare and cook a soufflé. Students answer and I know half of them are lying. When she turns to me I answer honestly.

"Fried chicken, meatloaf, and cornbread." I know it sounds simple, but we have perfected the recipes at the diner and have received nothing but praise.

"Nice and rustic," Taryn says.

I can almost feel the daggers Scott is throwing my way because of the attention she is giving me. I know he's chomping at the bit to brag. By the time she gets to him, nobody cares. She nods as he goes on and on. He gives her a bright, lopsided grin and winks. Holy shit, he's flirting with her. Sure, he is somewhat attractive, but how can she not see he's an ass? Plus, she is way out of his league. She looks at him for a few extra seconds and turns her attention back to the whole class.

"Soufflés are delicate, as most of you know. There is an art to it. Almost magic," she says. Her voice is fun and I find myself smiling at her playfulness. She is making a smoked mushroom soufflé and we watch her work, talk, teach. She's amazing. Since she is preparing food, she is wearing her chef's jacket and tall chef's hat. Her long, light brown hair is French braided out of her face and hits the middle of her back. Her hands are quick as she whips and explains her shortcuts, and her techniques.

"How long have you been cooking, Chef?" I ask.

"Since I was four," she says. I smile and picture a small girl standing on a kitchen chair scrambling eggs with Mom close by.

"What's your favorite thing to cook?" Scott asks.

"That's a hard question. I enjoy so many different things. I love the simplicity of omelets and the complexity of coq au vin. As long as I'm in the kitchen, I'm happy." Coq au vin is difficult because it requires braising a rooster, not a chicken, with a ton of other animal parts I'm not overly fond of, in a red wine sauce. Not my favorite thing to eat or cook. "A kitchen has endless possibilities and every day is a new adventure." She says the word adventure with an 'ah' at the end, and I struggle to stay focused on her cooking instead of her mouth. I wonder what she is like with a lover. Does her raspy voice drive him or her crazy? Does she talk during sex, whisper words of encouragement, or is she quiet and her mouth busy? I sternly remind myself to focus on her efficient technique, but my mind wanders over her slender body. She is taller than I am by a few inches, and has a body of a runner. She does her best to hide her slender waist and long legs under her clothes and her jacket, but it's hard to cover up perfection.

"Ki?" she asks. "Ki?" I look at her. I'm sure my face looks guilty, and I feel the heat of embarrassment color on my cheeks. I have no idea what she just asked or said to me.

"Chef, can you please repeat?" I ask.

"Is class not challenging enough today to keep your interest, Miss Blake?" she asks. I hear an edge to her voice and I know I've offended her. Shit.

"My apologies, Chef." She ignores me and asks another student the same question. I feel like an ass. I've single-handedly managed to bring down the mood of my instructor. Again. How is this possible? I've always been teacher's pet. I've even taught a class a time or two. So far, I haven't made a very good impression on Taryn. I know she approves of my cooking, but she's not impressed with the rest of me. I make it a point to stay focused on her lesson. I promise myself that I will make the best soufflé today.

When she dismisses us to our workstations, I plan a spinach, mushroom, and Gouda soufflé, adding just a little bit to her original recipe. She has given us free reign on what to add to our dishes, but since we have an abundance of mushrooms in the refrigerator, most of us are using them. I see Scott pull out a lobster tail and I can't help but roll my eyes. Both Mary and Taryn see me and for a brief moment I'm embarrassed again, but they both smile and the private moment shared between us gives me strength. I sauté shallots and mushrooms until the sizzling subsides, then add spinach, and try to recall Taryn's steps. I close my eyes for a moment and watch her fold the separated ingredients together. From memory, I follow the best I can. It's impossible for me to take notes in a kitchen. Cooking utensils only, not pens. I start the process and find I actually have enough ingredients to complete three attempts. I give a quick and silent prayer that one of them turns out and that nobody fucks with my oven. I stand guard over it and grab a cookbook Taryn has available for us to flip through. I about fall over when I see that the cookbook is actually her own. I'm trying not to put Taryn on a pedestal, but it's hard when she is obviously perfect. According to the book's forward, she was a finalist for a James Beard Foundation Award for the northeast two years ago. What the hell is she doing here in the midwest? Completely engrossed in the book, I almost miss my timer when it goes off. I'm not overly excited about my soufflés. One is overflowing, another is too dark because of the mushrooms roasting at the surface. The third has potential. I can't cover up the top with a glaze because obviously it's not a sweet dish. Instead, I decide to flash fry a few mushrooms and add them to the top. Not only will it add texture to the dish, but it will cover up the dark spots.

"Very nice, Chef." Taryn breaks open the soufflé. Thankfully, it is fully cooked. A few other students hang around to see my dish and congratulate me as well. "Nice use of the mushrooms on top." She takes another bite and savors the taste before she swallows. I can't keep my eyes off of her mouth. Her tongue darts out to quickly gather a few crumbs left by the last bite. Her mouth is generous and I wonder what it's like to devour it. I have an urge to reach out and run my thumb against her bottom lip, feel its softness under my touch. I know she has to be a fantastic kisser with lips as red and full as hers. "Thank you, Chef." Her words bring me back to reality. I find that I have moved somewhat close to her and I'm in danger of invading her personal space. I quickly nod at her and head back to my station. A few students congratulate me on my dish again. I can't even remember what I just made. The image of Taryn's mouth and what I want to do with it overtakes my thoughts.

CHAPTER FOUR

Saturdays at the farmer's market down in the River Plaza are a chef's dream. Cheap, organic, local food. I push myself through the week just to make it to the weekends so I can bargain with local farmers and growers for the best deals. I know several of the vendors. Some of them know me and save some of their better items, knowing I will buy from them.

I stand for a moment and enjoy the sounds and smells around me. Spices from around the world, flowers from local gardens, fruits and vegetables from farmers. I hear several different languages, mothers scolding children, and vendors singing to buyers. I can spend hours here. Today is my first Saturday off in a long time. I've been working at the diner on the weekends since Morgan had her baby, so today is my day of freedom. I immediately head for the spices. I'm most excited about them and they are the easiest to carry.

"Where have you been, pretty lady?" Akim asks. He smiles as I practically skip over to his vast array of spices. He has a permanent shop in the River Plaza and I stop in every time I'm here. I walk up and down the aisle, trying to figure out which ones I want.

"Stop flirting, or I'll tell your wife," I say.

"She knows I only speak the truth," he says. "What are you cooking this week?"

"That's just it. I don't know. I know I will need cumin and cinnamon. Do you have fresh rosemary this week?"

"Of course. I also have whole saffron." He whispers it to me as if we're sharing a secret.

"Shut up," I say. He nods. "Hook me up." After spending too much on spices, I reluctantly leave his stall and head for vegetables.

"Look what I have for you." I hear George yell from the second aisle, waving his arms to get me to his booth. I swear he has ESP and knows when I'm near. He holds up the largest eggplant I've ever seen. I head over to him, my brain already concocting recipes for eggplant a dozen different ways. My heart stops and I gasp when I notice Taryn picking through some zucchini and squash near George's stand. I'm completely surprised at the little girl who is holding onto the pinky finger on her right hand. The girl is adorable. She has curly, dark blonde hair and big brown eyes just like Taryn. Of course Taryn has a family. She's beautiful, smart, and can cook better than any chef I've ever known. I'm in a bad spot right now. This is her private life. It's always unnerving when you meet an instructor outside of the classroom.

"Hi," I say. Taryn turns to me with a surprised look on her face.

"Hi," she says. We stand there smiling at one another. I'm completely tongue-tied around her.

"You haven't been around in weeks, Ki," George says. I turn to him.

"I've been working weekends for the last month. Today is my first day off in forever," I say.

"You are too young to work this hard," he says. He bags three eggplants and hands them to me without even asking how many I want. "You should try slicing the eggplant thin, bake it, and halfway through, add some of your fresh herbs and spices." He points at my bag. Sounds simple and delicious.

"That sounds good, George. Thanks for the idea." I turn back to Taryn. "He has the freshest eggplants and squash around here. Do you come to the market a lot?"

"Olivia and I just moved to the area. This is our second trip down here. Olivia, meet Ki. She is one of my students." Olivia shyly sticks her forefinger in the corner of her mouth.

I squat down so that we are eye level. "Hello, Olivia. I'm Ki. Like pie."

Olivia giggles. "Pie? Your name is pie?" Oh, my God. She has a slight accent, too.

"No. Ki, with a 'K.'" I wink at Taryn. "C'mon. How cool is my name?"

"Almost as cool as mine," Olivia says. I laugh. She's a spitfire.

"Olivia is a very pretty name. You're the first Olivia I've met," I say. She smiles.

"What are you doing here?" Olivia asks.

"Probably the same thing you girls are doing here. Buying fruits and veggies." I stand up and am face-to-face with Taryn. She looks completely relaxed. Her hair is loosely pulled back in a ponytail. She's wearing a thin white oxford with the sleeves rolled up to her elbows and faded jeans. I wish I would have taken more time getting ready this morning. I'm wearing yoga pants, thin sweatshirt, and athletic shoes. My hair is also pulled back, but I'm a mess, and she looks great. Suddenly self-conscious, I quickly smooth down my hair and stop when I see her smile at me. She knows what I'm doing.

"You seem to know the area pretty well. Are there vendors we need to stay away from?" she asks. I'm surprised she's asking me for advice.

"Most of the vendors on the ends of each aisle are the best. They have the prime spots and have been here the longest. They also know their customers pretty well."

"You seem to be popular."

I smile at that. "I shop here all the time. Well, I used to before I got added shifts."

"So, why do you work at a diner? Your cooking is fantastic. You could really work anywhere." Her voice is so soothing and calming. It takes my mind a few seconds to process her compliment.

"Thank you, but I want to learn all types of cooking, and I really like it there. You should come by. Both of you. We are just down at the corner of fourteenth and Grand." I'm embarrassed. I just invited my teacher to my work. Now, we will awkwardly stand around until she says something non-committal. "No big deal. Just if you ever want to know why, come on down to the diner." I can't shut up. I will her to say something, anything.

"That sounds great. We just might do that."

"Can we go see the animals now?" Olivia asks. Taryn turns her attention back to her daughter.

"Can we pick up some fruit first?" she asks. Olivia thinks about it and nods.

"But we have to hurry, okay?" she says. "Come with us, Ki." It's more of a command and Taryn shyly nods her head in their direction, her invitation cute and playful. I am not used to this side of her.

"Hey, Olivia." She looks up at me. "Last time I was here, there were baby chicks. I even held them. They are so fluffy." She smiles at me and quickens her pace.

"Hurry, Mum." She tugs at Taryn's hand and zigzags us through hordes of people bartering with vendors in the aisles.

"Hang on, love. Let me pick up some apples and mangoes. Ki, any fruit vendors you like in this aisle since this is the only one I will get to?" Taryn asks. I just can't believe she's so relaxed. And beautiful. I notice other people glancing at her and I'm torn between being smitten and jealous. She mentioned she and her daughter just recently moved to this area. She didn't mention a husband, or a significant other. "Ki?"

"Sorry. Just trying to figure out where the good vendors are." Hopefully, I sound believable and she didn't catch me staring. She has to know I'm gay. Hell, Scott outed me on the first day of class when he accused me of flirting with her. I point to a farmer on the left and we head that way. Olivia drags her heels anxious to get to the animals instead of studying fruit with the adults. "How fresh do you want the mangoes? I mean, are you cooking or eating them right away?"

"Don't tell anybody, but we are going to work on mango glazes and chutneys in class so I need a few ripe ones now to practice with and several for Monday," she says. "Mangoes are fun and chutneys are easy. It will be a simple class."

"I have a mango chutney recipe that's fantastic. I serve it on the side with pork chops at the diner." She looks completely surprised. "This is why you need to visit the diner. Diners are completely misunderstood." Bud's Diner was created from love and it shows in his cooking. He's had several famous people dine at his place, and photos on the wall to prove it.

"We will. Let me know the next time you have a Saturday special that's spectacular, and we'll visit you there." I'm so happy I feel like I'm floating. My heart is racing like I'm on a first date, but I keep reminding myself that this is a chance meeting. Not only is she my instructor, but she's way out of my league.

"Finally." Olivia rolls her eyes. Taryn and I smile at one another. Taryn gives Olivia a few quarters for hay pellets to feed the goats and kids. Olivia has no fear.

"How old is she?" I ask.

"Six going on sixteen."

I nod my head in sympathy. "She's very cute. Very smart."

Taryn smiles at me. "She's quite the handful. But she's my entire life and I wouldn't have it any other way." I nod, not understanding if that's her way of telling me she's not interested, or if she's just opening up to me like a new friend. Taryn gets out her phone and takes a few pictures of Olivia feeding the baby goats. Olivia's delightful giggle is infectious and soon several bystanders are laughing with her.

"She's a ham, but completely adorable. She looks like you." I almost face palm myself at my stupidity. Rule number one: never, ever hit on your teachers. Not even subconsciously. Taryn's smile turns tight, and I know I've said something stupid. I'm not sure how to get out of this uncomfortable silence that seems to be going on forever. "So tell me where you're from. Both of you have accents." That seems innocent enough.

"I'm originally from South Africa, but moved to Florida when I was a teenager. I went back to Cape Town after college and was there for ten years. Olivia and I moved back to the United States about four years ago." She nods at her timeline.

"Wow. I've never met anyone from South Africa before. I was trying to figure out if you're from England or Australia. Well, you have a great accent." I cringe again because I still sound like I'm hitting on her. "I can tell Olivia has a slight accent, too."

"Hers will probably disappear over time. Mine won't," she says. I'm okay with that. "Honey, move your shoes away from the mama goat. She's trying to eat your laces." Her attention is back on Olivia. Olivia responds by dancing and moving around, squealing with a mixture of delight and alarm. "She's going to need another bath." We both watch in pure disgust as several baby goats nibble at her hands, their slobber webbing her fingers.

Olivia doesn't seem to mind, but I'm already trying to find the hand sanitizer. As a chef, I am constantly washing my hands. I hate for them to be dirty. I know the mentality of a six-year-old is different than mine.

"They have hydrants here somewhere. We can just hose her off," I say. Taryn briefly touches my forearm and laughs. She quickly pulls away as if my arm has burned her.

"I'm sorry," she says. And now things are awkward again. We turn our attention to Olivia, the silence heavy between us. I make a conscious effort not to look at Taryn, even though I'm very much aware of her nearness, her smell, her loveliness. I see her gradually relax again as she watches her daughter. "Olivia, it's time to go. Say good-bye to your new friends." Olivia starts pouting and I can't help but smile. It's amazing how much they look alike. She gradually makes her way over to the gate, slowly, making sure to pet each goat along the way.

"We need to come back here every week," she says matter-of-factly. She fusses a bit as Taryn douses her tiny hands with hand sanitizer. "And can we bring cookies for them to eat?"

"Sweetie, I don't think the mama goats want their babies to eat cookies. I think we'll just stick with the tiny pellets."

"Okay. But can we see them every weekend?" Olivia wrings her tiny hands hopefully. I'm nodding with Olivia, completely inserting myself into this family moment. I agree they should come back every weekend, not only for the great produce, but for the opportunity for me to bump into them again.

"We'll see," Taryn says. Both Olivia and I sigh. Everybody knows what that means. I try to lighten Olivia's mood.

"You know what, Olivia? Even if you skip a weekend or two, the babies will still be really happy to see you the next time you are here." She doesn't quite smile at me, but her frown is gone. "And if I'm here and you aren't, I promise to give them some food and tell them it's from you." Okay, score. That does it. She's happy again.

"Really? Do you think they will remember me?"

"Oh, I'm sure goats are like dogs. They will remember you and your smell. I'm sure you are stinky to them."

She giggles. "I am not."

I catch her smelling her arm. I point and laugh. "So maybe instead of calling you Olivia, I should call you stinky." She huffs, but can't help but laugh. Even Taryn is smiling. "Come on, stinky. Let's help your Mom get these fruits and veggies to the car."

"Thanks for your help, Ki. I appreciate it. This is a great market." I can tell Taryn is nervous, almost skittish around me. A part of me wants to reassure her I'm not going to jump her, but then I'm not entirely sure of that.

"You'll love coming here. There is so much to choose from and I always come up with new recipes every time I shop." We walk over to a black SUV and I help her load up the back while Olivia climbs into her booster seat. I lean into the window.

"Nice to meet you, stinky." I wave at her.

"Bye, pie!" she says. I look back at her with my best annoyed look. She laughs. She's just delightful.

"Have a good rest of your weekend, Taryn. I'll see you Monday." I leave them without a backward glance. I don't want Taryn to think that she affects me, and I don't want to scare her off because she does.

CHAPTER FIVE

I'm nervous walking to class. I know Taryn is already there because her car is in the parking lot. One of the great things about the culinary center is the layout of the classrooms. The first third of the classroom is a dry erase board and eight long desks. The rest of it is really a giant kitchen divided up into workstations for each chef. Each room has a glass front so that people can observe the instructors and students without disrupting class.

I hope to have a moment to watch Taryn before my presence is known. What I don't expect is Scott leaning over her pointing out something on her laptop. He is very close to her, too close in my opinion. The feral part of me wants to growl at him, partly because I see her as my friend now and I know he's a total slime ball, and the other part simply because I'm jealous. He's obviously interested in her. As I walk into class, Taryn looks up and we make eye contact. I can't tell if she looks guilty or annoyed. I raise my eyebrow and she gives me an eye roll. I shuffle my backpack around to cover up my relief and small burst of laughter.

"What's going on?" I feel like I need to say something since the three of us are in close proximity. Scott looks at me and takes a small step away from Taryn.

"I was just showing Chef a program on the Ethnic Food Festival this weekend. My family has a booth there. Everybody is invited." He smiles smugly.

"I'll probably go on Sunday." Not that anybody asked. "What is your family cooking?"

"Irish stew, soda bread, and a few other family recipes." That all actually sounds pretty good.

"I'll be sure to stop by." I pull out my chef jacket and put it on while Taryn and Scott discuss his menu in detail. I love that she is so interested in food, regardless of who's talking about it. I head to my station because I can't just sit around and stare at them. It's relatively clean, but I wipe it down again, anxious to stay busy and not watch them. I know we're working with mangoes today and I'm excited to see if Taryn will let us do what we want, or if we'll have to follow her recipe.

"Good news, Ki." Taryn is suddenly beside me and I jump, dumping the cup of soy oil I just poured all over the front of my jacket and onto the counter. "Oh, I'm sorry. I didn't mean to scare you." She's laughing and as much as I want to be mad at her, I can't help but laugh with her. It's nice to see her still relaxed and not in teacher mode yet. We both fumble around for paper towels to contain the mess. It's amazing how fast a cup of oil can spread.

"Well, you certainly got my attention." I look down at my coat, the oil stain is forming and spreading fast. I sigh. She grabs a few paper towels and runs them under hot water before applying them to the front of my coat. Without thinking, she starts unbuttoning my jacket. I watch her in complete stunned silence. When her fingers still, we make eye contact again. Her fingers are right at the buttons near my breasts.

"I'm so sorry." She takes a few steps back, both of us surprised at her actions. I finish taking off my chef jacket as if her hands weren't just on my body and my reaction to her isn't explosive. My heart hammers in my chest and I start to sweat. I swallow a few times, trying to think of a way to joke out of this, but I draw a blank. She heads over to the pantry and returns with a cup of white powder. "If you give me your jacket, I'll treat it with baking powder. It's the best and fastest way to get an oil stain out of clothes." I hand her my jacket with shaking fingers, hoping she doesn't see my reaction. If she does, she plays it off and works diligently on my jacket. "Grab another jacket from the supply cabinet." I need to get away from her so I quickly march over to the cabinet and slip on another jacket. I take a few deep breaths as I button it up and am able to calm myself. Other students start filling in the room and our moment, or whatever that was, dissipates. By the time I walk over to her, my nerves and my body have calmed.

"So, what's the good news?" I clear my throat, trying to lose the frog that has lodged itself tightly inside. She looks up from her project of cleaning my jacket, her eye contact almost fierce, confusing me further.

"Well, I was going to tell you that we are going to cook a protein with the chutney. That way you can make your delicious diner dish for me." Her face relaxes.

"This still doesn't release you and Olivia from the invitation of eating at the actual diner." I know I'm pushing her, but I feel like something might be happening here and I'm not ready to walk away from it. She finally smiles at me. "And don't worry about my jacket. I have a few of them."

"It's my fault you spilled it. I shouldn't have pounced on you." I lift my eyebrow up, acknowledging her choice of words. "Well, you know what I mean." She's actually blushing. "Anyway, I guess we should get started." I look up at the clock and sigh. This magical moment is over, but not forgotten.

"Chefs, today we are going to make a sweet mango chutney and I want you to prepare a protein you think pairs the best with it. And a side dish if you want extra credit." The class laughs at this because there is no such thing as extra credit, only over-achievers. I'm already mentally on it.

Taryn passes out the mangoes and starts her recipe. She explains why she chose the spices and ingredients she has and tells us that it can be made however we want. I'm eager to start mine, but watching her prepare is just as engaging. Now, I can actually stare and get away with it. After ten minutes of chopping mangoes, apples, gingerroot and adding spices, she starts the cooking process and excuses us to get started.

She has a small jar of chutney that she made over the weekend that we taste. It's fantastic. Almost as good as mine. I don't tell her that because I want to show her. I decide on an almond encrusted pork chop, butternut squash spaghetti with roasted vegetables, and my own mango chutney. Personally, I would love to make cheesy garlic mashed potatoes as part of this comfort food event, but she doesn't strike me as the mashed potatoes kind of girl. Maybe roasted potatoes, but nothing heavy. I take a moment and process my meal. What do I need to get started right away and what should I hold off on? I know there are no time restraints so I decide to pull together all of the ingredients first. I notice Taryn making her way through the class, asking each chef what they are cooking. By the time she reaches me, I've chopped my ingredients for the chutney, as well as the almonds for my pork chop crust.

"No starch, Ki?" she asks. I'm surprised she questions it.

"You don't strike me as the potatoes kind of girl." I wink at her. Why the hell did I wink?

"You never know until you try." She smiles at me as she makes her way to the next student. Well, shit. I can't help but grin. I'm stoked to make my cheesy garlic mashed potatoes now. Everybody at the diner loves them. Even Bud likes them and he doesn't particularly like garlic. I rethink my menu, replacing the fresh vegetables with my potatoes. I don't even look up for forty-five minutes. I know that people are starting to prep plates, but I'm in my zone and I don't want to leave my station.

"Who hasn't tried Mary and Tony's dishes yet?" Taryn asks. She's looking at me so I reluctantly head that way, two forks in hand. Both are good, just not thrilling. I do like the fact that Mary added slivers of peach to her chutney. Even though it's too sweet for me, the peach complements the mango nicely. I praise their dishes and head back to mine.

Somehow, I'm the last chef to turn in her dish. Only by a minute or two. Scott's dish was great, of course, so I had to step it up. My pork chops are fantastic. I found the best cuts in the refrigerator and cooked them to perfection. Pork is delicate, but I have worked with it enough to know how to cook it flawlessly. My potatoes are fluffy and my chutney is spot on. I can't help but smile as I bring my plates over to the rest of the class.

"Fantastic, Ki." Taryn smiles at me. The butterflies in my stomach are dancing, but I have to remain calm and professional. Scott even gives me props.

"This is really good," he says. He takes another bite of my potatoes. I can tell he is trying to figure out my ingredients. I'll never tell him.

"Thanks." I head back to my station to clean up. Class eventually files out and I'm left with just Taryn. I find myself taking my time, enjoying the few moments alone with her.

"You were right. Your chutney is amazing," she says.

"Thanks," I say. "I'm glad you let us pick a protein, too."

"Well, you gave me a good idea. I think all the students had fun today."

"We have fun every day. I can't imagine doing anything else."

"Have you always wanted to be a chef?" she asks. Oh, boy. She's going to love my story.

"Actually, no. I dropped out of law school. Surprised?"

"No, impressed, really. Just getting into law school is an accomplishment. When did you decide you wanted to cook for a living instead?"

"I've always enjoyed cooking. It's peaceful to me. Law isn't. There's no connection with anything. At least with food I have endless possibilities and they are all positive," I say. She nods. I slow down my movements as I clean up my station, talking and listening about her and Olivia. She looks up at the clock in surprise.

"Oh, my. I have to pick up Olivia." She jumps up from her chair.

"Go. I'll lock the door behind me. I'm almost done anyway." She thanks me and heads for the door.

"You did a great job today, Ki. I'm proud of you." She waves and leaves. What a fantastic Monday. Not only did I impress her with my chutney, but I kicked Scott's ass, and I got a few minutes alone with her. I'm starting to like the days of the week more than the weekends.

CHAPTER SIX

Y ou look great! Where have you been, girl?" Jessie grabs me in a big hug, squeezing me so hard that I grunt. I met her when I first moved into the building. She lives downstairs and has been my best friend since day one. I haven't spent a lot of time with my friends lately.

"I've been pretty busy with work and school."

Jessie holds my arms up and makes me twirl for her. "When was the last time you wore a dress and where have you been hiding these curves?"

I smile shyly at her. I rarely wear dresses, but today I felt like getting dolled up. We're going to an all day concert celebrating the LGBTQ community in the park and I want to look good. It's been a long time since I had a real date and maybe it's time to meet some new women. My everyday wardrobe consists of black slacks and white coats. I need color and style for at least one day.

"Stop. I'm just getting tired of my monochromatic wardrobe. I needed a break." I do like this dress.

"Well, lilac compliments you well," she says. I smile. It's been a long time since I heard somebody say something nice about me, not just my cooking. My hair is pulled back in a French braid. All day out in the sun, even though the temperature won't hit above seventy-five, will still be hot.

"I made us sandwiches, lemon bars, brownies, veggie chips, and some other stuff."

Jessie looks at the picnic basket then back at me. "You know there are only four of us, right? That basket must weigh a good twenty pounds."

"Then we can share with others around us." I put a lot of effort into our picnic. Jessie packed two bottles of wine, beer, and water. Sam and Lynn are responsible for the blankets and chairs. "Are we all set?" I don't even try to lift the basket. Jessie works out daily. Not only is she strong and beautiful, but she's tough. Her white T-shirt with a rainbow heart across the front is stretched tight against her chest and her cargo shorts hang dangerously low on her hips.

"Let's go." We head out to Jessie's Jeep Renegade where Sam and Lynn are loading everything up.

"Did you pack the entire cow in that basket?" Lynn asks.

"Just wait until you taste everything," I say. She grabs me and gives me a friendly hug. Sam isn't a hugger so she gives me an awkward wave three feet from where I'm standing. I smile and nod.

"Good to see you, Sam. How are you?" She's an IT manager at some insurance company downtown and doesn't have a lot to say most days unless it's about Zelda or other video games. I'm sure she feels the same way about my obsession with cooking as I do about her gaming.

"Good." She nods back. Okay, so we got through that. I climb into the passenger seat as Jessie loads up the basket in the very back.

"So what's the plan?" Jessie asks. I hand her the tickets and parking pass. The concert is about twenty minutes away. Our parking pass is pretty good, but we probably won't get a spot close to the entrance since we are three hours late getting there.

When we looked over the schedule last week, we didn't see any bands we wanted to hear until early afternoon.

"Let's get there, find a spot, and relax the rest of the day." I'm so ready to just enjoy my friends, the weather, and music. Jessie always has a rainbow flag that she stakes in the ground to help us find our way back to our blanket. With 10,000 people there, it's hard to remember where base camp is, especially if alcohol is involved. I plan to stay mostly sober because tomorrow I want to enjoy my Sunday and not be plagued by a wine hangover. I slip on my shades, lean back in the seat, and enjoy the sunshine on my face. I haven't felt this kind of peace in weeks.

Jessie gets us to the concert in record time. I end up carrying nothing. Apparently a woman in a dress is not required to lug heavy things. There are open spots about halfway up the hill and we head that way to set up and spread out.

"Ki! Ki!" A high voice calls. I turn and see Olivia waving at me. What the hell? What is she doing here?

"Hang on, guys," I say. I head toward her, waving. She gives me a quick hug when I close the gap, surprising me.

"What are you doing here, Olivia?" My mind is trying to process why she is at the concert. She has a NOH8 sticker on her cheek and looks adorable in her pink dress.

"Hi, Ki," Taryn says. She walks up behind Olivia, putting her hands on her tiny shoulders. I know my jaw is on the ground and there is nothing I can do to salvage any sense of coolness. Taryn smiles at me.

"Uh, hi," I say. I'm still in shock. My teacher is at a LGBTQ concert with her daughter.

"I'm here with a few of my friends," Taryn says. She thumbs behind her and I can see three other women lounging on a large blanket in the grass. I see a large cooler and am finally able to speak.

"You packed a giant picnic, too, huh?"

She laughs. "The outcome of being a cook and your friends asking you to whip up something for lunch." A small piece of hair blows across her face in the breeze and hangs up on her eyelash. Without thinking, I reach out and gently brush it from her face. We stand there for a moment, both of us looking at one another, neither speaking. I'm sure we are crossing a line here, but I don't know what the line is, or how far I should step over it. Before I can say anything, one of her friends is suddenly behind her.

"Can I get you anything, Taryn?" A slender and beautiful woman with short brown hair comes up behind her and Olivia. I don't miss the possessive gesture as she puts her palm on Taryn's back. I look down, then back up at Taryn. She looks a bit angry and I don't know if it's directed at me.

"No, thank you. We are good here. Mallory, this is Ki, a friend of mine. Ki, this is Mallory." She doesn't specify their relationship so of course, I think the worst. The worst for me, obviously not for her. I nod at Mallory.

"Nice to meet you. Have you all been here long? Have we missed anything?" I try to keep the conversation light. I still can feel Taryn's smooth skin against my fingertip and try hard to keep from staring at her. My desire for her is always close to the surface and it's getting harder and harder to hide it. Mallory decides to be a wealth of information and tells me everything I've missed and how they have such a great spot. I'm already tired of her. I squat down to talk to Olivia who is getting antsy from not being involved in the conversation.

"What about you? Are you having a good time?" I ask. She reaches out for my hands.

"Can I come with you and your friends?" she asks. I smile. She probably doesn't like Mallory either.

"Maybe later once we get set up and I know where we are and if it's okay with your mum," I say. Olivia starts jumping up and down with excitement.

"You don't have to do that, Ki," Taryn says.

"If you aren't comfortable with me having her, I understand." I can't help but be somewhat disappointed that she doesn't trust me with Olivia.

"It's not that." She reaches out and puts her hand on my forearm. "I just don't want to ruin your time with your friends." She's not moving her hand from my arm, something I'm very much aware of. So is Mallory.

"They love kids. We'll get settled and I'll come back and get her in a bit if that's okay." She nods and Olivia whoops with excitement. "Okay, stinky, I'll see you in a bit." Olivia smiles.

"Bye, pie!" I smile and walk back to my friends who have been waiting for me.

"Who are those people?" Jessie asks.

"Holy shit. That's my teacher and her daughter, and some other people I don't know," I say.

"That hottie is your teacher?" Jessie asks. She whistles low. "Damn. I get why you have it bad for her." I nudge her forward so we can get away from Taryn and I can collect myself. I need to process that my teacher is a lesbian. Class is going to be one hundred times harder now that I know. Not because I think I have a chance, but because I don't. Mallory made that perfectly clear. My emotions are teetering on a high wire, threatening to crash all around me. Today is not the day to wallow in self-pity. Today is a day for my friends and maybe finding somebody for me. That was the plan. Now I'm not so sure.

"Oh, and later I'm going to bring Olivia back to hang with us, so drink up your wine now. It's water when she's around," I say.

"Hey, if it helps you get her mom, we'll drink water all day," Lynn says.

"Unfortunately, I think she's taken," I say.

"If you aren't one hundred percent sure, then she's still available according to the Lesbian Handbook, page eighty-one, paragraph two," Jessie says. That makes me smile. She's great about cheering me up.

"Hey, how about that spot over there?" Lynn points to a place that's fairly open. It's close enough to the bathrooms, but not too close, and close to the vendors. We head that way and spread our blankets out. Jessie stakes our flag and a few people clap and whistle. It's a tad obnoxious and hopefully doesn't block anybody's view, but very easy to see.

"So, I know you said your teacher was pretty, but wow, Ki." Jessie plops down next to me.

"Yeah, quite a surprise that she's here."

"You never had a clue? Not one?" she asks.

"No, trust me. I would have flirted more if I thought so."

"No, you wouldn't have." She nudges me with her shoulder. "You're too career focused to throw it away on a beautiful woman. Isn't it against all school rules everywhere to have sex with a teacher?"

"It's not like we're in high school." I'm defending something that hasn't even happened.

"Well, try not to think about it too much. Just look around you. There are beautiful women everywhere." She opens up her arms and does a sweep of the crowd. "Look at that girl over there. She's hot," Jessie says. Okay, now I'm pretty sure we're scouting for her.

"Let's eat. Who's hungry?" I'm not in the mood to prowl. I'm not very hungry either, but I need to do something to occupy my mind. The girls are pretty excited to eat so I hand out chicken salad sandwiches and homemade sweet potato chips. They seem happy as they munch away.

"I think you're a fantastic cook and I can't wait to run your restaurant for you," Jessie says. She has management experience, but not the kind I'm looking for. My own restaurant is a long way away, and life will change for both of us by then.

"Thanks, Jess. Too bad my mom doesn't feel the same way."

"Stop. She's proud of you even if she doesn't say it all of the time. Once you win the scholarship to Italy, you'll forget she ever doubted you."

"I don't know about that. She's still pretty pissed at me."

"At least you got scholarships through school and still have a chunk of your trust fund. It's not like you are a financial burden to her."

"So, your mom is mad at you for becoming a chef?" Sam asks. "Does she know how good your cooking really is?" I smile at Sam. That's the most she's ever said to me.

"Thanks. She's still upset that I dropped out of law school to attend the culinary academy. I think she liked bragging about her daughter becoming a lawyer. Hard to make a chef sound good to your friends."

"Our moms are old school," Lynn says. "My mom still isn't happy I'm gay. It's just their generation. Don't worry about it."

I nod. At least my mom is okay with me bringing home girlfriends. I just haven't done it since college. I think she's worried there as well.

"Well, I'm going to go get Olivia so drink up your wine and pull out waters. I'll be back in a few minutes." I stand up and straighten and smooth down my dress. Jessie stands up next to me and wipes a few crumbs off of my cheeks and then pinches them. "Hey." I smack her hands away.

"You are entirely too pale. You need a little color," she says. I playfully push her away from me and head back to where I think Taryn and Olivia are sitting. I'm know I'm getting close when I spot a tiny person twirling in a circle just to my left. I see Taryn sitting down near Olivia, her arms out just in case Olivia falls. I clear my throat and walk toward them.

"Ki! You came back," Olivia says.

"Of course. I said I would, right?" She hugs me again. "I love your dress. I wish it came in my size. Are you hungry?" She nods.

"She just ate lunch so she's probably only hungry for sweets," Taryn says. She's looking up at me, her hand shading her eyes from the sun. "I'll walk her with you so that I know where you're sitting." I want to help her up, but I can actually feel Mallory's hard stare so I don't dare reach out for Taryn's hand. "Everyone, this is my friend Ki. You've already met Mallory. The other two ladies are Carrie and Sarah." I nod hello. They seem friendly enough. "I'll be right back." Taryn doesn't wait around, but grabs Olivia's hand and walks in the direction I point. I quickly slip in behind her.

"Who's your favorite musician here?" Not the question I want to ask her, but it's a start.

"Catie Curtis, but there are so many other great singers." Since we are single file, she slows down to answer me and I bump into her. I put my hands out to steady both of us, but not before feeling her curves against mine. Today, she is not hiding beneath a chef jacket and boring black slacks. Today, she's in shorts and a tank with a lightweight shirt over that. Her wedge sandals aren't very practical for this environment.

"Thanks for the catch."

I point down at her shoes. "Lose them. You'll twist your ankle." She nods and leans down to take them off. She reaches out and uses my arm to steady herself in the process. For ten seconds, I feel the strength of her fingers against my skin, her warmth burning into me and spreading throughout my body. The urge to touch her is growing at a pace I can't control anymore. She smiles after her shoes are off, and we continue walking toward the giant rainbow flag. "See? Our picnic is easy to find." My friends are sprawled out, listening to the music, and don't see us approach.

"Guys. This is Taryn and her daughter Olivia." I introduce each of my friends and I'd laugh at their reaction if I wasn't already nervous. Jessie, always the gentlewoman, jumps up to say hi. Lynn smiles and Sam, of course, waves.

"It's nice to meet Ki's friends," she says. I watch each of my friends fall under Taryn's spell. "This is a great concert. I'm going to have to make myself come to more of these."

"Mum, may I have a brownie?" Olivia asks. Jessie almost sighs at Olivia's accent. Taryn looks at me for approval. For a second, I get lost in her eyes. We are so close that I can actually see tiny freckles on the bridge of her nose and little dark flecks in her eyes.

"Of course." Olivia doesn't hesitate and helps herself to the largest brownie on the plate. "Would you like one, too? And please sit for a minute. I don't want to be in everybody's way." The girls shift positions and the three of us sit down on the blanket.

"You have a great view of the stage from up here," Taryn says. She breaks off a piece of Olivia's brownie and takes a bite. My whole body is tense. She hasn't tried my desserts before and even though brownies seem simple, I'm always trying to find a way to improve them. I've made Dulce de Leche brownies for the first time.

"These are fantastic, Ki." She moans with appreciation. Jessie winks at me and I smile a thank you at both of them. "The sea salt is perfect."

"I usually get that part wrong," I say.

"Not this time," she says. She reaches for another piece of Olivia's brownie, but Olivia moves it away. "And apparently Olivia thinks so, too."

"So you like Ki's cooking, huh?" Jessie says. "She's very vague when she tells us how class is going." I can feel myself blush.

"I can understand why Ki is still in the running for the scholarship," Taryn says. I can't hide my smile. "Although, she does have some pretty stiff competition." My smile turns into a frown and everybody laughs.

"No, it's true. Scott is a great chef. If he only remembered to slow down, he would totally beat me," I say. Taryn winks at me. My smile is back. "I'm not giving up that soon, though. I still have a few tricks up my sleeve." I'm flirting and Jess gives me a subtle thumbs up.

Jessie starts up a conversation about South Africa with Taryn and that gives me a private moment to study my teacher. We are sitting side by side and if I lean closer to hear their conversation, I can feel the heat radiating from her body. She is leaning back on her hands, her long, slender legs curled up near me. They are shapely with tiny freckles sprinkled on the tops of her thighs. She is fit, but not too muscular. I'm surprised at how relaxed she is with my friends. She reaches for the brownie that Jess hands her after Olivia denies giving her another bite. Out of the corner of my eye, I watch her taste it again, her eyes closing for a moment as she savors it. I love watching her eat. She has an appreciation for food, too, and I know that she is thinking about the ingredients and how they harmonize so well together in a single bite.

"I'm going to need your recipe." She smiles at me. When her tongue darts out to catch a crumb, I swallow hard. My eyes dart down to her mouth, admiring her full lips and pink tongue.

I want to kiss her. I want to feel her heat, taste her passion, glide my hands possessively over her body until we both clutch one another with desperate need. I grab a handful of the blanket to keep myself from doing something stupid.

"Whatever you want," I say. Jess leans back and raises her eyebrow at me. Yeah, that sounded like a bad pick up line. "I mean, sure. I can email it to you later this weekend." She smiles at me, but this time it's a different smile. One I can't really identify, but with an element of wickedness to it. Her phone buzzes with a text message that I can see, but not read. She gives a slight sigh.

"Well, I guess I'm going back to my party. Ki, take my number and let me know if there is a problem, or you want me to come and get Olivia," she says. Jess tosses me my phone and I hand it to Taryn.

"Go ahead and add yourself to my contacts." I would do it myself, but I'm afraid she will see my hands shake. I watch as she quickly types in her name and number and hands the phone back to me.

"Olivia, be sweet with these ladies. Listen to them and don't wander off." Olivia is smiling, but nods her head in agreement.

"Yes, Mum." She digs around in the picnic basket for something else to eat. Her mother leaving is apparently not a big deal. Taryn's having a more difficult time parting.

"Don't worry, Taryn. We'll take good care of her. There are four of us and only one of her. We've got this. No worries," I say. Taryn smiles and nods. I watch her walk away, my heart finally slowing down for the first time since she joined us.

"What are these, Ki?" Olivia's question yanks me out of my daydream. She is holding up a sweet potato chip, inspecting it as if it has something on it that might be distasteful. Knowing that she will balk if she knows it's a vegetable, I make something up.

"It's a twisted, thin cookie with cinnamon sugar. You should try it," I say. She's still unsure, so Jess grabs one out of the bag and pops it in her mouth.

"Yum! Give me yours." She grabs at Olivia's hand. Olivia squeals and eats it before Jess gets it. She chews for a bit.

"These are weird, but good." She reaches for another one and happily munches away, her tiny body wiggling back and forth.

"Don't eat too many. I don't want you puking on my blanket," I say. She laughs at me, but I know enough about little kids to know that rich foods will make them projectile vomit without warning. I encourage her to drink water to stay hydrated and full. Eventually, she relaxes and snuggles up next to me. She's humming and pulling at the grass. She asks me kid questions like what superpower would I want to have, and if I could be a princess who would I be. Within a few minutes, she is zonked out. I can't move so I just sit there and listen to the music and my friends talking. This is surprisingly peaceful. I grab my phone and take a pic of Olivia and send it to Taryn. I'm not in the picture, but it's obvious that she's up against me. I quickly get a text back.

She's already asleep! That's amazing. Want me to come get her?

She's only been gone for half an hour. I can't tell if she's nervous for me or for Olivia.

No. Let her sleep. Enjoy your baby-free time.

I don't want to think about what she's doing right now. I don't want to know that her head is resting in Mallory's lap, their fingers entwined, enjoying the closeness that lovers do. I know that I should be happy she has somebody, but realistically my heart hurts. I should leave her alone, but now that we've opened up this form of communication, I can't help myself.

Catie is up soon. Are you excited?
Very much so.

I'm pronouncing her texts with her accent as I read them. I keep the conversation going. *Are you staying for the whole concert?*

Probably not. Olivia needs to get to bed at a decent time even though it's Saturday.

I don't know if we will stay until the end either. J gets antsy, especially if she meets somebody new.

Oh, I thought you were together…

My heart stops. She thinks Jessie and I are girlfriends. *No. I love her but she's not my type. I'm single.* I groan. I can't believe I said that.

What's your type?

I freeze. I can't believe she said that. I sit for a moment. My stomach is quivering and I'm excited. Is she flirting with me or just being inquisitive? *A bit more girly and mature.* I convince myself that is an acceptable answer and hit send.

"What are you doing? And why do you look guilty?" Jessie asks.

"I'm texting Taryn."

"Oh? And what might you ladies be discussing?"

"Nothing really. I sent her the photo of Olivia." I don't want her to know about our texting because then she'll be hounding me for information, or scolding me.

"Mm hmm. Well, just remember she is still your teacher for two more months."

"I know." I know this more than anything. I know I don't really have a chance with her, but it's still nice to dream. I wait for her response, but she is quiet so I put my phone down. When Catie Curtis takes the stage, I'm tempted to send her a text, but I don't. Olivia stirs against me, the noise and the clapping waking her up. She is tired though and fighting to go back to sleep, but the newness of me and the others keeps her from it.

"Where's Mum?" She rubs her eyes.

"Do you want to go to her now?" I ask. Her big brown eyes are expressive. She thinks about it for a long moment, then shakes her head. "Do you want to go see what kind of stuff they have for sale over there instead?" I point in the general direction of the vendor tents. She smiles.

"I want a lemonade," she says.

"Olivia wants a lemonade so we're going to head out. Say your good-byes," I say. Jessie's fist bump makes Olivia giggle. She waves at Lynn and Sam and grabs my hand, leading the way. "Be back in a few." I'm surprised that they have games behind the vendors including a ball toss game, bean bag game and darts. Naturally, Olivia wants to play all of them so we manage to kill another twenty minutes showing one another how horrible our aim is. Hers is excusable, she's six. I have no justification. The dart attendee gives Olivia a tiny pink elephant for trying and winks at me as I thank her. She tells me to come back later if I have time.

"Now can we get a lemonade?" she asks, one hand clutching her new stuffie, the other holding my hand.

"Do you want pink or yellow?" I ask.

"Pink!" She squeals with delight. I'm pretty sure I know her favorite color. I hand her a souvenir cup with a silly straw. She gives me the elephant to hold so that she can still hold my hand.

"Let's go find your mum," I say. I head to where I think Taryn is, hoping my sense of direction gets us there. She waves at us, already looking our way before we see her.

"Did you have fun?" Olivia hugs Taryn's waist, her tiny face nodding against Taryn's shirt.

"I fell asleep though," she says.

"Thanks so much, Ki. Do you want to sit down with us?" I can see Mallory looking at us again.

"Thank you, but no. I should get back. She's such a sweet girl." Taryn looks surprised that I don't want to sit with her, but the look Mallory is sending me isn't very welcoming.

"Bye, stinky," I say. Olivia gives me a quick hug.

"Bye, pie," she says.

"Well, thanks again. I'll see you Monday, I guess." Right now Taryn and I are standing awkwardly in front of one another. I want to hug her, but I know that if I touch her, I will think of nothing else the rest of the weekend.

"Okay, have a great rest of the day." I don't know what else to say so I turn around and leave. I know that she is watching and I wish that she would follow me, but I know she either can't or won't.

❖

"I'm glad we left early. Can you imagine how bad the traffic would be if we waited until the end?" Jessie says. There is something lethargic about all day concerts. For doing absolutely nothing, we're all exhausted.

"Thanks for driving, Jess," I say. Both Lynn and Sam chime in thanking her, too.

In a surprising turn of events, Jessie didn't hit on a single woman today. We arrive at the apartment complex, and all of us say our good-byes and scatter.

I have just enough energy to put away the remaining food before crawling into bed. Sophia greets me warmly and refuses to let me sleep. I snuggle with her and wonder what Taryn is doing. I'm still in shock over the fact that she is a lesbian. I can't tell if this is a test for me. I decide I want to be in a serious relationship with a mature woman and all of a sudden we have a new instructor at the academy who is beautiful, whose cooking makes me want to weep with joy, and is a lesbian. Is she a gift or a punishment? How serious is her relationship with Mallory? I can't imagine it being fantastic if Mallory is so protective of Taryn. I'm not a threat to them. At least I don't think so.

CHAPTER SEVEN

"S o you thicken the sauce with crushed up ginger cookies?" I'm standing in front of a German booth at the Ethnic Food Festival eating a tiny piece of sauerbraten, a pressure cooked braised beef in thick, rich gravy. I'm in love with all of the wonderful flavors. The lady running the booth, Sonja, whose last name I couldn't remember or pronounce if I tried, is telling me her recipe.

"Yes. Add them when you are boiling the broth," she says. I'm not too familiar with German cuisine so every little bit of advice helps, and her version of this dish is delicious.

"Thank you so much. This is very good." She answers me with a smile and nod. I'd love to sit and talk to her more, but other people want samples and I've already had two so I reluctantly leave her booth. I know Scott's family is around here somewhere.

"We do have German food on the syllabus." Somebody says near me right before I feel somebody else grab me. I look down in surprise to see Olivia's hands hugging my waist. I turn to see Taryn behind me, Olivia nestled between us.

"Hi, ladies. What a nice surprise." I mean it. My smile is larger than it should be for just a chance meeting so I try to tone it down.

"German food is basically proteins and starches. The good stuff is in the sauces," Taryn says.

"Isn't that true with most foods?" I say. She winks at me. I melt and swallow hard. To distract myself from her, I squat down so that I'm even with Olivia.

"Are you tasting everything here?" I ask her. She crinkles her nose at me.

"No. Just the sweet stuff."

"Olivia isn't much of a taster. If I think she'll like it, she will at least try it."

"It smells funny in here," she says. Taryn and I both laugh.

"I couldn't agree more, Olivia." Too many different types of food packed into a convention hall. Spicy, sweet, sour, pungent, mild. Unless you know what you're smelling, it isn't entirely pleasant when mixed together.

"At least they have something mild at most of the booths," I say. This festival is a family affair and to keep the kids happy, most booths have a cookie or sweet item that is relatively bland for the kids to try. It still introduces them to a new food, just on more kid-friendly terms.

"Like she needs any more sugar. She's had enough this weekend to last her a month."

"We should have sugar at every meal," Olivia says.

"Then you wouldn't be healthy and would weigh a thousand pounds," I say.

"Okay, but a little bit of sugar?" She holds up her tiny forefinger and thumb with about an inch gap between them. I reach over and pinch her fingers closer together, closing the gap by half. She giggles and agrees.

"Have you seen Scott's booth?" I ask. I don't want to talk about yesterday. It's hard to keep eye contact with her today because I know about her now. I'm afraid I will read too much into any look she gives me, or any small touch she places on my skin. I need to keep this casual and fun.

"No, but since we are in Europe over here, he should be close," she says. We end up walking together, tasting foods and discussing ingredients and what we like, love, and could live without. Her palate is remarkable. I try not to watch as she tastes the samples, but everything about her mouth is so arousing that it's hard for me to look away. I wonder what it's like to kiss such perfection. I want to touch her lips, run my fingertips over their softness, taste the smoothness against my rough tongue, scrape them against my teeth. My thoughts must be visible because she stops chewing and stares at me. It's a curious look mixed with surprise. I turn away and focus on Olivia.

"You should really try this," I tell her. The Cornish meat stuffed pastry from the England booth is not really kid friendly, but I need to focus on something else. Olivia smells it and shakes her head no.

"Too much meat for her. She's not really a fan. Plus it's kind of spicy and she's not ready for spicy yet."

"What is her favorite thing to eat?" I'm glad we have Olivia as our buffer when things get uncomfortable. She's a safe and fun topic.

"She likes cheese pizza, macaroni and cheese; a lot of the food found on most children's menus," Taryn says.

"Do you ever cook her food from South Africa?" I ask.

"Some. It's a bit spicy and she's not a fan of curry really. She will eat chicken and peanut stew, milk tarts, and a few other things. I'm afraid my mother spoiled her with American food when she started eating solids." I find out that Taryn's mom is from Connecticut and her father is from South Africa.

"So why did you move here to the United States?" I ask.

"More opportunity here for me and for Olivia. Better healthcare, better schools, better restaurants. I learned so much when I arrived."

"Do you see your family a lot?" I ask.

"My parents helped me get set up in my new place a few months ago. Mum is supposed to be here again in a few weeks. As far as us going to visit them, we might see them on our summer holiday, but it depends on the academy's schedule. They miss us, but they understand this is what's best for the two of us. Mum promises me that they will retire in the United States. She wants to be involved in Olivia's life while she grows up. I guess I need to figure out if I want to stay here or move." That surprises me.

"You would move? I mean, teaching at the school is fantastic, right? We've learned so much from you already." I hear the panic in my voice and settle down.

"Well, although I do enjoy teaching a lot, I really want to be an Executive Chef again or even own my own restaurant. This schedule works best for me because of Olivia. When I worked at Rally's, I never saw her. I worked from three until eleven and she was already asleep by the time I got home. I would only get a few hours of sleep before I had to get up and take care of her. Now, even though she's at school and in Adventure Club after school, we are on a normal schedule. It's just the two of us and I can't rely on my neighbor to take care of Olivia all the time."

"I understand completely. She's a great little girl." We fall silent and continue walking down the aisle. Taryn has already sacrificed so much to have a life with Olivia. My admiration for her has just jumped a level.

"Taryn! Taryn!" We both see Scott waving at us. I love how he's ignoring me.

"Hello, Scott," she says. He smiles at her, the charm elevated. I smile because I know it's wasted energy on his part.

"Hi, Scott," I say with a bit more sarcasm than pleasantry. He smiles at me, but it's not the same kind of smile.

"Come here, Mom. Meet my teacher," he says. A sweet, round lady comes over to us.

"It's nice to meet you. I've heard many great things about you." She's very nice and I wonder if she knows her son is an ass.

"You have quite the chef on your hands," Taryn says. I walk away from the exchange. It's obvious Scott isn't going to introduce us and I don't really care. My attention is on the food they've cooked for the event. It smells great. I reach for a small portion of Colcannon, a dish of mashed potatoes and cabbage. It's a simple dish, but seasoned very well. The Irish stew is even better.

"Ki, Ki. Will I like that?" Olivia looks at the stew.

"Want a bite?" She opens her mouth so I feed her a small bite of the mashed potatoes.

"How do you know Taryn's daughter so well?" Scott asks. He comes up out of nowhere.

"Mum and Ki are friends," Olivia answers for me. I don't know what he's trying to get at, but I make sure he knows she's not playing favorites between us.

"I've seen them at the farmer's market a few times," I say. "I just ran into them over in England." I point to the other aisle and do my best to look bored. He looks at me skeptically. I change the subject. "How's the traffic been? Are you getting a lot of visitors?"

"It was steady yesterday. Today is more hit or miss."

"Everything I've tried at your booth has been very good. Kudos to you and your family." Flattery will hopefully get his mind off of why I'm close to Taryn and Olivia.

"I can tell my parents are getting bored. They are used to hustling in the kitchen every day, not sitting down at a booth. This will hopefully get more business to their restaurant."

"Well, it's a good restaurant. Maybe we should have a school field trip there. You should talk to Taryn about it," I say.

"Good idea! I might do that," he says. I slowly let out a sigh. He's moved on from us and back to him.

"Okay, see you tomorrow." He dismisses me and returns to Taryn. I need to leave so that it doesn't appear we are at this function together. Neither of us needs that grief. I head over to where everybody is standing.

"It was nice to meet everybody and taste your wonderful food, but I need to go," I say. I pretend to be in a hurry so I give Olivia a quick hug and kind of shrug at Taryn when she gives me a look. "Bye." It sucks that I have to miss the aisle where foods from Russia and China are, but leaving is more important for all of us involved.

❖

I'm sitting on my balcony with Sophia, both of us enjoying the last of the day's sunshine. My feet are up on the railing and she is sprawled out on the other chair. My phone buzzes, drawing my attention away from the book I'm reading.

Why did you leave so quickly?

My stomach does a flip-flop and I hold my phone for a few moments, excited that Taryn has texted me again. I decide to tell her the truth just in case it comes up later. *Scott asked how I know Olivia so well. I didn't want him to think we spend a lot of time outside of the classroom together.*

There is a pause before I get her response. *That was considerate. Thank you.*

I know she's not being sarcastic, I'm just surprised she doesn't ask me anything. *He can be a jerk.*

This I know already. Really, thank you.

I know I should stop texting her, but I want to keep this connection with her. *I wanted to stay though.* Okay, so maybe that was a bit too raw right off the bat. I quickly send another text. *I like hanging out with you girls.* I can't hit send quick enough and actually hit the button several times. I stare at my phone and wait. Again, a long pause.

Olivia says hi. She wants to know who I'm talking to.

I breathe a sigh of relief. I didn't scare her off. *Hi, stinky. What are you doing?*

I laugh. I better qualify that statement. *I mean Olivia, not you.*

Lol. I figured as much.

I can tell that I have this goofy grin on my face, but nobody can see me so I don't care. Taryn's next text is a photo of Olivia's smiling face. She's so damn cute! I decide to send her a photo of Sophia sunning next to me. Sophia looks up at me when she hears the camera snap. Bored with me after only two seconds, she yawns and settles down.

Olivia loves your cat. She said she can't wait to have a kitty.

I got lucky with Sophia. She's the easiest cat around. I'd have a dozen cats if that didn't make me look a little crazy. Plus my apartment lease only allows me to have two cats at a time. Sophia is perfectly happy being single. Me, not so much.

Park time, bath time, story time, and then bed time. Olivia says good night.

Have fun and tell her to sleep well. See you tomorrow.

I don't get another text so I put my phone down and pick my book back up. I read the same sentence over and over before I finally give up. I feel like I have something here with Taryn. Something that could be more than friendship.

CHAPTER EIGHT

Maybe it's my imagination, but I think Taryn is early to class so that we have some time together before the other students show up. I'm almost always the first student in, but today she is already here. I refrain from skipping to class even though the desire is great. She looks up and smiles at me. My heart swells with excitement and slight fear. What if I'm reading too much into this, whatever this is?

"Hi." I slow my pace as I walk through the door. She looks fantastic. Her hair is down and pulled over one shoulder as she takes notes from something she is reading on her computer. I've noticed lately that she is wearing a little more makeup and she waits to put on her chef's jacket. All the signs are there. If I didn't know about Mallory, I would say she's interested. Or maybe she just likes the attention I give her. Either way, I'll take it. I like this relationship we have in secret.

"Hi, yourself," she says. Her voice is warm and I just want to melt into her.

"What's on the agenda today?" I casually walk over to my desk to drop my bag, then make my way over to her.

"Tenderizing meat and four ways to do it," she says, wagging her eyebrows at me. "We'll figure out what method works best for different proteins."

"Should be fun. Do we each get a protein and method, or will this be a group project?"

"What do you think?" She's actually asking my opinion.

"It might be faster if we group up. I mean, we can do more in less time if we are in groups."

"Good idea. What proteins should we work on?" I'm surprised she is involving me this much. I like it. We chat about meats for a few minutes before Scott and a few others arrive, breaking our tranquil closeness. Taryn sighs when the students walk in and I take a step away from her feeling guilty without reason. I head to my station and clean it up, trying my best not to seem affected by our short time together. I can feel Scott staring at me so I decide to chat with him and throw him off a bit. I head his way with a casual smile on my face.

"How did the rest of the festival go?" I sound genuine even to myself. I see his shoulders relax.

"It was good. There was a rush not long after you left. Thank God there wasn't a lot to clean up. I think we'll get more traffic at the restaurant now."

"I really liked the stew. Your parents have a great recipe there. Let me guess. It's a family secret."

He laughs. "Something like that." The rest of the class starts filing in so I head back to my station, glad to be away from him. Taryn starts class and I find myself instantly captivated by her. I like watching her work. She's so delicate, yet works quickly and efficiently. I have so much respect for her after knowing that she gave everything up to raise her daughter. She was Executive Chef at the nicest restaurant in town and chose to walk away from it to be there for Olivia.

"Marinades are a great way to tenderize a protein."

Even though I'm listening to her instruction, I'm focused on her. Not what she's saying, but her. I'm watching her mouth, fixated on her smooth and red lips. She chews on her bottom lip while concentrating on showing us a technique. She looks up quickly and makes eye contact with me. For a second or two, she freezes. I try to pretend that she's just my teacher and I'm just a student, but I think I'm past that. I think she must be past that, too. Something flickers in her eyes. It's a mixture of surprise and desire. I don't look away. Not this time. Not after everything the past few weeks. She stutters for a moment, but recovers quickly.

"Okay, well let's get into teams of four and decide on a protein and a way to tenderize it." She clears her throat and completely avoids eye contact with the class. Scott and I automatically pair up with other students, knowing that it doesn't make sense for us to be on the same team since we are in competition with one another. Mary is on the third team. Even though she is still technically in the running for the scholarship, she knows she is too far behind us to win. Nobody talks about it, but we all know.

My team decides on steak. Since we don't have six to eight hours to allow the meat to properly marinade and tenderize, we decide on beating it. It's a quick way to get the meat tender and I can get out my frustrations on a piece of meat.

Class flies by, but I still can't get out of there fast enough. Not only did our team come in last, but Taryn managed to ignore me the rest of the afternoon. Not a single word spoken to me. I know the fact that I was staring at her probably threw her off, but I know I'm not the only one who has ever been caught. I clean my station, grab my bag, and get the hell out of there. The farther I get from the academy, the easier I can breathe, but the heavier my heart feels. I still have almost two months to go and I have to find some sort of peace with Taryn. I can't lose the possibility of the scholarship all because of a crush. I need to figure out how to squelch my desire for her and keep it on a friendship level. I snort at myself, knowing that's going to be next to impossible.

❖

"Want to go out for an ice cream or something?" Jess is on the phone trying to get me out of my funk. We met downstairs in the foyer when I got home and she must have picked up on my melancholy mood.

"No thanks. I'm cuddling with Sophia tonight." Sophia is sitting on my chest staring at me while I rub her chin.

"Want to just veg and watch the game?" I know she's trying, and it's not as if I'm going to be doing anything special tonight, so I cave and invite her up. She opens my door in five minutes, holding cold beer and popcorn.

"So what's going on? Why do you seem sad?" She plops down on the couch, prompting Sophia to spring off of my chest, her nails thankfully retracted. I sit up and take a beer from her outstretched arm.

"I don't know. This whole Taryn thing is just eating me up. I get mixed signals from her. I know she's gay, but I also know she's with someone, so maybe I'm reading too much into her actions. Does that make sense?" I rub my forehead and try to relax. Maybe Jessie will have something profound to share with me.

"Has she said anything to you yet?" she asks.

"Meaning?"

"Has she hit on you, asked you out, made it clear she's interested? Do you think you could be reading too much into it just because you know she is a lesbian?" Jess asks. Too many questions. I groan in frustration.

"No, she hasn't said a single thing, although she did ask if you and I are together," I say.

Jessie almost spits out her beer. "When was that?" She wipes beer from her mouth onto her shirt. If I tell her the truth, then she'll know we have been texting. Not a lot, but an open form of communication that is always there if I need it.

"Today. Before other students got to class." I don't want her to know yet.

"How did it come up? Did you talk about Mallory?"

"No, she just asked me if we were together, that's all. Don't you think that's weird?" I ask.

"Because of me, or just weird that a teacher would ask you that?"

I laugh. "Not because of you, dork. Maybe that she even asked at all. Usually people who do are interested."

"And maybe you're dreaming." She nudges my knee. "Seriously, unless she asks you out, or gets you in a dark corner and kisses you senseless, better just assume you two are only friends. Keep it teacher-student until the semester is over."

I sigh. "I know. It's just that I feel like there is something there, or could be something there, and I don't want to miss it because I'm reading the signs wrong."

"How about once you receive your certificate, you walk up to her and ask her out. Better yet, offer to make her dinner. From now until then, think of the most perfect meal you could cook for her. Just for her. If Mallory is there, I'll distract her and you can make your move." She winks at me and we toast our beers. It's a dream, but kind of a fun one.

CHAPTER NINE

S o my teacher and her daughter might show up today."
Bud and I are grilling up breakfast early Saturday
morning. I picked up Morgan's shift so that she could visit her
in-laws with the new baby. I don't mind.

"So that's why you have such a spring in your step." Bud
high fives me. I can't stop smiling.

"Be nice to her when she gets here," I say.

He waves me off. "When am I ever not nice?" I snort. Bud is
almost three hundred pounds and well above six feet tall. When
he's not smiling, he looks like he's posing for a prison mug shot.
"Well, okay. I'll be charming and nice. At least to her daughter."
I'm thinking once he sees Taryn, he'll be even more charismatic.

Breakfast is a breeze. I know the menu by heart. I'm more
excited about lunch. I brag enough about my fried chicken, so I'd
better deliver.

"Hey, quit blocking the doors," Ashley says. She's trying to
deliver a few last minute breakfast plates and I'm face planted
against the windows looking out into the diner, waiting for Taryn
and Olivia. I scoot over so that she can open the door.

"Sorry. Just waiting on somebody." She winks at me.
Everybody knows. Another good thing about the diner. We really
are a tight knit family.

"I promise to let you know when they get here. Pretty girl, cute kid. I got this," she says. I smile and get back to the kitchen. It's almost lunchtime, so I heat up the deep fryers and start prepping the chicken. Bud's making my rosemary parmesan roasted potatoes and after careful consideration, we decide on garlic creamed spinach as the vegetable side. It's a bit upscale for normal diner food, but Bud knows our customers will like it. I take a moment to tune everything out and get into the zone. Once I hit it, I forget about the hustle and bustle around me. I add a dash of paprika for extra sweetness and kick, and start blending the small ingredients into the flour. I start frying chicken as the orders come in, Taryn and Olivia momentarily forgotten. I'm pleased with the crunchy skin and juiciness of the meat.

"Ki," Ashley says. I look up at her, still in my zone. "They're here." My stomach lodges in my throat. I swallow hard. Nope, still there. I take a quick drink of water and wash my hands.

"Quick, how do I look?" I ask her. She straightens out my jacket and wipes flour off of my cheek.

"You look fantastic. They've ordered their drinks. I'll go get them, you go say hello." She marches back through the swinging doors and I get a quick glimpse of them before the doors settle. Olivia is on her knees on the bench coloring. Taryn is reviewing the menu. I know she probably isn't impressed yet, but that will change the minute she tastes the food. I take a deep breath and walk through the doors.

"I'm glad you two made it," I say. Taryn smiles at me warmly.

"Hi, pie," Olivia says. She's so cute. It's hard not to reach out and squeeze her.

"So, your famous fried chicken, eh? With interesting sides for a diner," Taryn says.

I smile at her. "They cater to my whims on occasion. I hate it when they have corn on the menu. Who eats the corn? Like two grandpas in this town actually eat the corn. It's such a waste," I say. She laughs.

"So garlic creamed spinach is better?" She winks at me.

"Well, maybe not with the kids, but the adults like it. Olivia, are you going to eat my chicken, or do you want me to make you something else?" I ask. I can feel Taryn watching me as I interact with Olivia. My peripheral picks up her looking me up and down. I don't think I've ever been more self-conscious.

"Can I have a hot dog?" she asks. "And some fries?" I just shake my head at her.

"Really? I can cook you anything you want and you decide on a hot dog?" She giggles at me. "You don't want to try my chicken?" I already know it's too spicy for her, but it's fun teasing her.

"You can have a bite of mine," Taryn says. "I guess she'll have the hot dog and fries and I'll have the fried chicken special." She raises her eyebrow at me.

"You can't grade me here, Chef." Suddenly, I'm doubting myself.

"Oh, stop. You've been talking about the diner and your fried chicken for so long that I had to come here and taste it for myself." Ashley shows up with their drinks so I nod and slip away, anxious to get their food started.

"So, they showed up, huh?" Bud asks.

"Finally." I push up my sleeves a bit and set out to tackle a few more orders ahead of theirs. When their orders come up, I pull the best chicken I can find, ensure that it is properly coated, and gently place it in the fryer. The potatoes are still hot and fresh, so we only have to wait on the chicken. I say a little prayer that it cooks perfectly and work on Olivia's meal. Hers only takes a few minutes. We get a lot of children in on Saturdays since kids' meals are half price all day.

The chicken looks crispy and delicious when I pull it from the fryer. I pick the best looking potatoes from the pot and wait for the creamed spinach to drain a bit before plating. I don't like my foods to touch. I think that's common for most chefs. I quickly make a French fry tepee for Olivia. Everything looks great. I'm careful when I deliver the food, hoping Taryn doesn't see my hands shake when I put the plate in front of her.

"Wow, Ki, this looks fantastic," Taryn says. I watch as she turns the plate, looking at the components. "Good coloring, great smells." I want to sit down with them, but I know it's rude. Besides, she hasn't invited me. Olivia is beside herself over the tepee.

"Can I eat this?" she asks.

I laugh. "Of course. I was just having fun in the kitchen. Well, enjoy. I'll come by later." I casually head back into the kitchen and do a little dance behind the doors. I peek through the round windows again and watch both of them dig in.

"Is it going to be like this all day?" Ashley asks. She's trying to get around me again. Even though she's acting perturbed, I know she is just playing with me.

"Just until they leave," I say. Bud comes up behind me and looks out of the window.

"That's her?" he asks. I nod and sigh. He gives a low whistle. "I sure hope your chicken is good today." I elbow him and am rewarded with a grunt. "Come on, we've got more orders to fill." I reluctantly leave the window and return to the fryer. When things slow down, he motions for me to go. I can't get out of the kitchen fast enough. I slowly push the doors open and walk over to their booth. I see Taryn's clean plate and give a silent whoop of joy.

"So, what did you think?" I ask.

"Fantastic. Well worth the trip down here," Taryn says.

My smile is huge and I don't care. "Did you like your hot dog?" I ask Olivia.

"I liked the chicken better," she says.

I roll my eyes exaggeratedly. "I told you."

"Can you sit with us?" Taryn points to the extra spot next to Olivia. I slide in the booth, gently knocking Olivia. She giggles. I'm so in with this kid.

"Okay, give it to me straight. Likes and dislikes," I say.

"Love the crunchy and tasty skin. The meat was juicy and tender. Spicy with a hint of sweet. The potatoes were crispy on the outside, soft on the inside. And the spinach was excellent. Right amount of garlic and the almonds added a nice texture to the dish." I kind of want to reach over and high five her, but that seems immature, and I'm doing my very best to impress her in every way I can.

"In all fairness, Bud made the potatoes."

"But your recipe, right?" she asks. I nod. "Very good meal. I'm almost positive I don't need to eat dinner tonight. Incredibly filling."

"So you're Ki's teacher?" Bud walks over to us. He introduces himself to Taryn, instantly charmed by her smile. Olivia looks scared. I want to crack up at her, but she'll figure him out soon enough. "And who might this little beauty be?" He leans toward Olivia and she leans into me.

"He just looks mean, but he's a teddy bear, trust me, Olivia," I say. I introduce them and Olivia eventually warms up to him.

"Ki's been telling me how wonderful your diner is and how much she has learned from you," Taryn says. I think Bud actually blushes. I'll tease him about it later.

"She's taught us all so much here," Bud says. Now I'm the one blushing. They discuss recipes and I sneak back into the kitchen to fill the rest of the orders since Bud is in no hurry to get them done. Another fallen victim to Taryn's charms. I can't blame him or anyone really. She's spectacular.

CHAPTER TEN

H i." I know it's Taryn calling so I'm not even going to pretend.

"How are you?" She sounds sad.

"I'm okay. You don't sound good. What's wrong?" Her little laugh sounds strained and I'm struck with a heaviness that makes me sit down. Whatever is bothering her isn't good. "Does this have anything to do with why you were late to class today?"

"I'm afraid it does." She sighs and I lean back in my chair, bracing myself for whatever she is going to say. "So, apparently some people don't like the fact that you and I have a friendship. I've been accused of playing favorites and I was told that we couldn't be friends anymore. Teachers and students can be friendly, just not friends." I'm stunned. I don't know what to say. "Ki? Are you still there?"

"Uh, yeah. I'm just processing it all." I'm so mad right now. "What did they say exactly?"

"Just that we shouldn't spend time together outside of the classroom."

"It was that little prick Scott." I'm livid. I'm actually shaking. "He's so threatened by me, by us, that he wants any edge he can get. What an asshole." A part of me wants to cry. Nothing has happened between us, but now he's made whatever could happen impossible.

"I think it was him, too. Nobody has seen us out together except for him." She sighs.

"Did you get into trouble?"

"No, not really. More like a slap on the wrist. They are bringing in another instructor or someone to taste food just to make sure my marks match the food the scholarship students are preparing."

"Are you kidding me? That's ridiculous." I'm so mad. "We haven't done anything wrong. We just happened to be at several places at the same time. Scott sucks."

"That just means you'll have to be the better chef from here on out."

I'm not even worried about the scholarship at this point. "I'm sorry if I got you into trouble, Taryn. I just enjoy spending time with you and Olivia. I know you're in a relationship and I want you to know that whatever you need me to do, I'll do it. You are the best teacher I've had at the academy and I don't want to jeopardize anything for you."

"That means a lot to me. You're a great student and a good friend. When the semester is over, I will cook us dinner to celebrate your graduation, possible scholarship, and the resumption of our friendship." My heart sinks. I'm not ready to let her go. Whenever I see her, my breath catches and I feel my heart race. She is trying to make me feel better about this, but it's not working. "And it's only for six more weeks."

"I know. Well, try not to let this get you down. I will cook my heart out and make you proud."

"I'm already proud of you." We sit there in silence for a few moments. I don't even know what to say at this point.

"Okay. I guess I'll see you tomorrow. Take care."

"You, too." I hang up. I want to find Scott and kick his ass for being a giant asshole. I hate being accused of something that isn't true. Injustice is one of my biggest pet peeves. I feel my phone buzz.

I'm not in a relationship.

I read the message over and over again. My heart is pounding, the sound loud in my ears. Why would she tell me this? *You aren't with Mallory?*

No.

Well, she wanted the world to know that you were together at the concert. I can almost feel our relationship changing as I wait for her response.

Yeah, and that was obnoxious. I don't bring anybody I date around Olivia.

Do you date a lot? Ha ha ha. I have to keep it light because if I read too much into this exchange then I will slip and fall hard.

No. I haven't dated anybody in a long time. Mallory thought she was my date but she was with my friends. I wasn't happy at all at the concert. Only when I spent time with you and your friends.

My friends are pretty cool. Maybe when school is over we can all get together for a picnic or barbecue.

I would like that. Her text makes me smile.

Bring Olivia. She's sweet.

We should make your friends cook. Taryn doesn't know how spoiled my friends are. I can't imagine they would jump at the opportunity to cook for two chefs.

LOL that would never happen.

After about half an hour of texting, I reluctantly say good night. I'm exhausted mentally and physically. Not to mention that I still don't know where our relationship is. Are we still on the safe side of friendship, or have we approached the line that flirts with deeper emotions?

CHAPTER ELEVEN

I keep my distance at school just to make everybody happy, except for myself. Dr. Wright, the culinary administrator, has been lurking around, watching the classes from the lobby. It's hard to pretend not to know why he's there, but I do my best. I don't want Taryn to get into any more trouble because I'm the one with the crush. Scott is just a complete asshole. Every time I see that smirk on his face, I just want to rub food all over it, and not in a good way. Taryn's also taking a step back. She gives me very little attention in class, and what she does, seems forced. I'm sure nobody really notices it, except the three of us. The only real satisfaction I get is that she completely ignores Scott unless it's culinary related. He's finally getting the hint. I take great satisfaction in knowing all of his attempts at flirting and charming Taryn are for naught. After a week of virtually zero communication with Taryn, I cave. It's Friday night, and I am on my couch petting Sophia, listening to sappy music, and flipping through a month old gossip magazine.

I hate Scott. It's a simple text, but sums up everything nicely.

Thankfully, she responds right away. *I know. He's not my fav either.*

I smile. At least she understands. *What are you doing?*

O and I are watching a movie. She's about ready to fall asleep though.

What movie? I'm on the couch with Sophia reading a mag.

Mary Poppins. It was my favorite growing up.

Our texts are nice, but too much time passes between them. I know she's busy with Olivia, so I pout and turn on the news. My phone rings fifteen minutes later. I freeze when I see her name on my phone.

"Hi. How are you?" she asks.

"Okay. Happy you called me." I cringe at my honesty.

"Well, it's faster than texting. I'm not great at that. It's a generation thing," she says.

I laugh. "We're the same generation. You're probably only a few years older than me. What are you? Thirty-one?"

"I'm twenty-four." We both laugh. "I'm thirty-six going on eighty because I have a six-year-old who is aging me."

"She's adorable."

"She's inquisitive. She's at the 'why' stage of life. Mummy, why does it rain? Why does it thunder? Why is the sky blue? Why? Why? Why? I might have to go back to school just to keep up with her."

"That just means she's creative. She wants to learn things. At least she isn't like a lot of kids who only want to play video games all the time. And she's crazy about swimming, right? Do you have a pool?"

"She's taking swimming lessons at the community center. We live at Walnut Grove and a few pools in the complex are getting ready to open up. This is a good place for us for now. I'm waiting to see if the academy is the right fit for me before I buy a house."

"Walnut Grove is a nice place." I know this because when I was looking for an apartment, I pulled up all available ones near the academy and that complex was way out of my price range.

"It really is. Olivia doesn't care that it's not a house. She loves the nature trails, the pools, free movies on Sunday nights in the theatre."

"I live on the other side of the academy. If this apartment building is part of a complex or has a nice name, I don't know it. I think it's just an apartment building. I still have to take my laundry down to the basement to do it. It does have loft ceilings and a cute little balcony."

"I'm sure it's nice," she says.

I want to extend an invitation for her to come over once school is out, but I think it's too soon. I'm just thankful she called me tonight. Not talking to her for days was unbelievably hard. We talk for another two hours about cooking, our favorite books, music, television shows, and fashion. She likes my purple dress from the concert. It's too bad that I can't wear it to class. After stifling several yawns, I reluctantly say good night and wish her sweet dreams. I can hear her smile over the phone.

❖

Work is steady and smooth. Even though I was up late talking to Taryn and got little sleep, I'm in a great mood. It's a beautiful spring day, everything is in bloom and I'm getting stir crazy.

"What's going on with you? You're like a busy little bee," Bud says. I shrug like it's no big deal that my heart feels happy and my brain won't stop thinking about a certain teacher.

"I'm just feeling good today. I think I'll even hit the farmer's market after work." I hope that I run into Taryn and Olivia there, but I doubt it. Most of the good stuff is gone by early afternoon.

"Make sure you reimburse yourself for all the stuff you bring in here," Bud says.

I wave him off. "You feed me every day. It's the least I can do." I'm rewarded with a giant hug.

"Go on, get out of here. We've got this," he says.

I check with Ashley and Val who agree with Bud. Traffic is light in the diner this late in the morning. I grab my things and head out, anxious to get on with my weekend. Sunday is my only day off and when my Saturday is short at the diner, I feel like I'm getting a full weekend.

The first thing I do is pick up lemons and a few limes. I'm going to make a lemon merengue pie to celebrate this beautiful day. Jessie will come up and help me eat it, I'm sure.

I walk past the petting zoo, sad that Olivia isn't inside, playing with the baby goats and other farm animals. I wonder if she knows there are lambs today? I should at least text that to Taryn. I take out my phone, snap a photo of a lamb, and hit send. I am rewarded with a photo of Olivia squeezing that very lamb.

You were here today!

We still are.

My heart beats faster. There are a lot more people here today because of the nice weather. In case she is watching, I play it cool and casually look around before I respond.

Are you close to the animal pit?

I see you.

Now she's messing with me. *Not fair. Where are you?*

Our eyes meet when I look over at the ice cream parlor. She and Olivia are drinking lemonades in the shade. Olivia is playing with a jewelry set, not paying attention to me. I have a quick and private moment with Taryn so I drop my special smile, hoping it works. I see her eyebrow hitch ever so slightly, and her smile back to me grows. I head their way, careful to keep my pace slow and steady.

"Hello, ladies," I say and casually lean over the railing.

"Ki. Oh, I mean pie. Hi!"

"Stinky. What are you making? Is that a bracelet? Is that for me?" I ask. I see Taryn looking me over. Thankfully, I'm wearing capris, a cute button-down short-sleeved shirt, and sandals. I look like a normal person, not somebody who's been working a grill all morning.

"How was work?" Taryn asks. I focus my attention on her. She's so beautiful and I feel my breath catch just looking at her. She is wearing a tight T-shirt and jeans. I wish she was standing so I could get a better look at her.

"Unusually slow so I decided to come here."

"Good choice. Come sit with us."

"Are you sure?" I'm afraid somebody will see us, but she nods her approval, so I walk around the railing and slide into the open seat.

"Would you like a lemonade?" she asks.

"I'll get one in a minute," I say. She waves me off and gets up. I shake my head at her and watch her walk up to the counter, enjoying the view of her ass in her tight jeans.

"Ki? Here I made this for you." Olivia interrupts my lustful thoughts about her mom. She hands me a bracelet with charms of little unicorns and flowers.

"For me? Olivia, that's so sweet. Can you put it on me?" I ask. She struggles getting it on my wrist, but she's patient. Taryn returns with a lemonade and places it in front of me.

"Thank you."

Taryn winks at me. "I thought you were making that for me."

"Mum, I will make you one tonight," Olivia says.

"Well, I guess that means Ki is pretty special for you to give her a bracelet," Taryn says. Olivia nods. I smile at the exchange.

"It's because I made you a French fry tepee, isn't it?"

She laughs at me. "No."

"It's because I won you a stuffie at the concert, isn't it?"

She laughs even harder. "No."

"It's because I'm awesome, isn't it?" She nods. I shrug at Taryn.

"When you've got it, you've got it." Taryn toasts me with her lemonade. "What are your plans for the rest of the day?"

"I was going to whip up a pie with these lemons. That's about it."

"Olivia and I were going to walk around the lake at our complex and feed the ducks. Would you like to join us?"

I hesitate, but only for a second. "Is that a good idea?"

"I think it's better than hanging out here."

"Sure. I'll pick up some oats and meet you at the complex." She texts me her address and we head our separate ways. I take my time finding oats for the ducks because I don't want to appear desperate. After giving them a fifteen minute head start, I find my car and drive to Walnut Grove. This place is gorgeous. I head to their building and climb the steps up to the second floor. Olivia opens the door almost before I knock.

"Where have you been? We've been waiting for you." She grabs my hand and pulls me inside.

"I had to find the perfect oats for your ducks," I say. I hand her the bag.

"Why can't we just feed them bread?" she asks.

"It's not the best thing for the ducks. It's not healthy for them," I say. She seems satisfied with that answer.

"Come on in, Ki," Taryn calls from the kitchen.

"Your place is beautiful." With the exception of the child artwork on the refrigerator, there are no other signs that a child lives here. The light couches are clean and bright with giant fluffy pillows everywhere. Everything has a place.

"Thank you. Shall we get going?" Taryn asks. Olivia is politely hanging onto the doorknob, anxiously waiting for us to leave. The walk down to the pond is peaceful. Olivia is ahead of us, skipping and twirling while we take our time getting there.

"What do I do with the oats?" Olivia asks.

"Take a handful out and throw them over the water," I say.

She drops most of the oats at her feet the first time, but by the third attempt, she's got it down and the ducks are swimming at attention in front of her.

"Don't get too close to the water, Olivia," Taryn says. She points to a bench closest to the pond and we sit. I give her enough space, but I can still feel her body heat. I would give anything just to touch her. As nice as this afternoon has been, being this close to her is killing me.

"I love that you do so much with her."

"Well, I don't have very many friends here. Not that I would stop doing things with Olivia, but it's nice to go out and do adult things once in awhile."

"I know what you mean. I have friends, but I don't have the time. Plus, a lot of my friends are young and still want to party. I'm so over that."

She nods. "You're at that age. I was like that, too, in my late twenties. By twenty-nine, I knew I wanted to have a child before I was in my thirties, so I found a donor and made it all happen." So that answers the question about Olivia's father.

"I was wondering about her dad," I say.

"Just a friend from college. He signed off on all parental rights."

"So how come you didn't wait to start a family until you found the right person? If that's not too personal. I mean, you are an attractive, successful woman. Why not wait?" I know I'm kind of pushing her, so I sit back and wait.

"You're kind. I'm not perfect. I had Olivia because I'm selfish. You know how demanding our field is. My relationships have been very difficult to keep. Nobody works our hours or understands our passion. I was tired of waiting, so I decided to start a family on my own. I mean, my parents helped, but ultimately Olivia was my choice." She leans back on the bench and crosses her arms defensively.

"I'm sorry. I didn't mean to upset you, I'm just curious about you." I try to backpedal and do damage control.

She sighs. "It's okay. It's just hard balancing work, a personal life, and a family life. I don't want a lot of people around Olivia, so it's hard to try to have a relationship." She has to know I'm interested in her. I want to tell her just how much she affects me, how desperately I want to be with her. Instead, I wimp out and stay silent. I still have to work and learn from her for the next five weeks. I can't go down this path unless I know the outcome.

"Well, I'm positive that everything will work out for you once you get settled at the academy." I try to keep the sadness out of my voice, but the look she gives me tells me she hears it, too.

"I'm out of oats." Olivia walks back up to us. I can't tell if her timing sucks or it's the best thing ever.

"It's probably time for swimming class anyway," Taryn says. She scoops Olivia up and sits her on her lap. "Did you thank Ki for the oats?" Olivia shakes her head.

"Thanks, Ki."

"Thanks for my awesome bracelet and you're most welcome for the oats. Just remember that oats are safer for the ducks, okay?" She nods. "Okay, go swim like one of your ducks. I'll see you soon." I stand up and Olivia reaches up to me for a hug. I make it quick because that puts me entirely too close to Taryn. I quickly say good-bye and wave them off when they offer to walk me back to my car. I need to put distance between us. Maybe today wasn't such a great idea.

❖

We had a good time with you today.

The ding of Taryn's text snaps me out of a catnap. Sophia and I are cuddled down on the couch.

I keep my response light. *I always have fun with you both.*

I'm sorry this is happening. I hate that we have to hide our friendship from everybody.

I frown. I think this relationship is taking a different direction than just friendship. *Is that what this is?* My heart speeds up. I wait a few seconds before I hit send. I stare at the screen, waiting for her to send me anything. Thirty seconds goes by before I see her typing.

That's what this has to be for now. Her answer sends chills all across my body. I haven't been reading too much into our playful banter after all.

I want to see how far I can push her. *So you are saying that if we met anywhere other than school, we might have something other than friendship?* I'm so still right now, clutching the phone, waiting for her response.

We can't talk about this. It's not fair to either of us. Well, that's not a no, but not a resounding yes either.

Okay, goodnight. I will see you in class. I end the conversation. Upsetting her isn't my goal. I just want to know that we have a chance, even if we both have to wait.

CHAPTER TWELVE

W hat are you doing here so late?" Taryn asks.
Concern is etched on her face. It's ten thirty Thursday night and I'm standing outside of her apartment door. I'm tired of wanting and waiting. We have a month left until graduation, but I know I can't wait that long. Her messages the other night seemed encouraging so I decide to throw caution to the wind and see what happens if I tell her how I feel.

She doesn't invite me in. Leaving her door ajar, she steps into the hall, keeping her back against the wall. She's in a tank top and tiny shorts and I take a moment to look at her. She waits for me to answer. I lick my lips with nervous anticipation. I want to say so much, blurt out my feelings, but now that I'm in front of her, I'm completely frozen.

"What's the matter?" she asks.

I feel like she is challenging me, waiting for me to make the first move. It's now or never. I step closer to her so that we're only a few inches apart. I can feel her breath on me, feel heat radiating from her body. Without shoes on, she is only about an inch taller. I hesitantly reach out and cup her chin, running my thumb just under her lip. She doesn't pull back. She just watches me. I've made the first move. I'm going to have to make the second one, too. Slowly, I lean forward and kiss her. For a split second, I feel hesitancy on her lips, and just as I am about to pull away with embarrassment, I feel her react. That's all it takes. I push her up against the wall and kiss her with everything I have. My hands are wound in her hair, holding her close to me. I feel her hands on my elbows either to steady herself, or touch me. I feel her with my entire body. Her hands slide down to my waist and hold me closer. Her small breasts are firm against mine. I can feel her hard nipples through her thin tank top. I desperately want to taste more of her. Here, in this cold, brick hallway is not the place to seduce her though. I break the kiss, almost smiling at the look of disappointment on her face as I pull away.

"Let's just have one night together. Nobody will ever know." I kiss the corners of her mouth, waiting for her to invite me in. I slide my hand down her body until we are holding hands.

"Ki." Taryn squeezes my hand, but makes no move. I don't know if she is thinking about it or trying to let me down gently.

My confidence leaves. I swallow hard as I realize this night is not going to turn out how I want it to. I take another step back, and loosen my hold on her hand. I miss her warmth already. I swallow hard. "I'm sorry. I shouldn't have come."

I give her fingers a squeeze and slowly make my way down the hall. She doesn't stop me and it takes all of my strength to not run away. I don't even look back. My heart is breaking and I need to leave before she sees my tears. I slowly make my way down the stairs. Once I'm out of her line of vision, I cry. I don't actually sob until I reach my car. What was I thinking? How stupid of me! Now we will never go back to the quaint friendship I had with her and Olivia. I completely ruined that. How am I going to face her almost every day for four more weeks? I'm such an idiot. Class will be one hundred times more stressful. Not only will I have to cook the best food ever and try to maintain top seed for the scholarship, but I have to act as if that very passionate kiss did not happen. I have to see her as an instructor and nothing more. I can't look at her mouth and remember how sweet she tastes or look into her eyes and see all of her emotions swirling around. No, I have to forget about this entire semester except for the techniques I've learned from her, and get started on the rest of my life. Four more weeks of pure hell.

❖

Sleep was fleeting, at best. I played the count game. If I fall asleep right now, I will get five hours, no four, no two hours of sleep before I have to get up and start my day. At least it's almost the weekend. I just have to motor through work this morning and through class this afternoon. After checking the syllabus, I find that next week we will be working at a few different restaurants. Thankfully, I won't be confined with Taryn in a glass box, visible to all. I'm not sure how I'm going to be able to keep my emotions hidden from everybody, including myself.

I grab my clothes for work and stumble around. I don't even think coffee is going to help me, so I head straight for a caffeine explosive Monster energy drink. Not the best way to start my day, but it's the only way to get through it. Work won't be bad. I just have to go through the motions, fry up some eggs, and get lunch started. Then, I have to go to class. My heart tenses up and fills with sadness. This is an ache I am unfamiliar with and wouldn't wish on anyone.

By the time I make it to work, I'm fully caffeinated, but still heavy hearted. Most of the staff can tell I'm not having a great day and leave me alone. I manage to screw up a few orders before Bud takes over on the grill, shooing me off to go prep for lunch early. Even he knows something is wrong, but is wise enough not to ask.

"Shouldn't you be on your way to class by now?" Bud points his spatula at the round clock on the wall. Yep. Definitely. I don't want to get there early though, so I take my time gathering up my stuff. Of course the traffic is light and I still make it to the parking lot ten minutes early. I sit in my car and wait until two minutes before the start of the hour to head inside. Taryn is there, scrolling on her laptop and the rest of the students are preparing their work stations for today's lesson. I set my bag down at the back of the class and head for my area, my chef's coat already on. I don't want to have to stand two feet from her to put my bag at my desk. She looks up when she hears me, but doesn't say a word. I can't even look at her. I give a nod in her general direction and quickly gather up my cooking essentials before she starts.

"Since we're all here and since it's Friday, let's have fun." Her accent almost makes me smile. "I think we should bake today. I know most chefs don't like to make desserts, but it's important to at least know how to make a few things from scratch." Out of the corner of my eye, I see Mary smile. I might as well throw in the towel now. Scott is about as happy as I am. He's worse at desserts. "Let's make macarons." Several students groan.

"But I thought we were working on rubs today," somebody whines.

"I'm allergic to coconut," Scott says. Mary rolls her eyes at him. Even I know the difference.

"Macarons, not macaroons. The colorful, round cookies that can be made a hundred different ways. You're safe, Scott," Mary says.

"It's Friday and I want to try something different. We tried desserts earlier in the semester and most of you struggled with them. Rubs are easy. Cooking meat is easy. Macarons are not. Plus, you can take them home and eat them over the weekend." She starts off explaining two different ways to fold the ingredients together. One is dry, the other is wet. My brain takes over and I start playing the role of student again. Taryn is quick, but informative and we're all glued to the lesson. She makes the syrup and points out the importance of temperature. While we wait for it to heat up, she beats the egg whites until they form soft peaks. Once the temperature of the syrup is constant, she adds the mixture to the egg whites, keeping the steady whipping action while folding the ingredients together. It is amazing to watch her work. She never doubts herself. She is sure, confident, and beautiful. Wait. My heart starts to beat faster as it pushes my brain in a direction I don't want it to go. Last night's memories wash over me and I have to hold onto the counter to ground myself.

For a few glorious seconds last night, she kissed me back. There's no denying it. I felt her against me, felt her hands on my waist as her fingertips slipped under my shirt for a brief, wonderful moment. There is something between us. Something bigger than that kiss. I just need to wait until the semester is over and I can either explore it, or get away from it.

By the time she dismisses us to our stations, I'm still somewhere between final whipping stages and food coloring. I have no idea what to do after that. Maybe by then, instinct will take over and I'll be able to finish them without asking for help. I've gone the entire semester without her assistance. I'm going to look like I'm trying too hard if I ask now. I don't want to be around her. I don't want her around me. I go back to my station and close my eyes for a moment to think. I need to find the zone. I'm perfectly still for I don't know how long until I feel a nudge. I turn to see Mary looking at me.

"Are you okay, Ki? You've been standing still for about five minutes now."

I stare at her for a moment, thankful she bumped me into action, but upset that I still haven't found my zone. "Yeah, I'm just retracing the steps. I can't remember what happens after the food coloring."

"Just take a third of the meringue and blend it with the almond mix. Fold it together until it's smooth, slap it in the pastry bag, then it's done."

"Thank you so much, Mary. I owe you." I'm filled with excitement as I figure out the last few steps in my head. Got it. Zone found, cookies to be made. I tune everybody out and start. A lot of cooking and baking is about timing. If you learn how to manage your time in the kitchen, you can accomplish so much.

I put my earphones in to avoid talking to anybody who might feel the need to converse, specifically Taryn. Although everybody is ahead of me, I'm holding my own. I carefully fold the ingredients together, heat them on the stove and begin my meringue. Other students are giving me looks, probably because my music is loud, but I ignore them and finish beating the egg whites. Half of the class is already baking the cookies, some have to start over, but I'm right on task. I add my syrup at the exact temperature and mix the two together until the frothiness stiffens. I quickly add pink food coloring to the mix and can't help but smile as color explodes in the bowl. Olivia would love this particular shade of pink. It's bold, not pastel, and I hope that doesn't ding me. I fill my pastry bag, add parchment paper on the sheet and start making small discs. They smooth out nicely without blemishes. Their tiny perfection makes me smile for the first time in a long time. Somebody taps my shoulder. I look up to find Mary peeking over my shoulder.

"Those look beautiful." I pull out the earbuds and stare at my accomplishment before putting them into the oven to bake. Mary really is sweet. She made purple macarons and even added a bit of lavender to her ingredients. Smart girl. I can't wait to taste them. She leaves to make her buttercream frosting and I decide on a ganache filling. Might as well go out with a bang.

Dr. Wright slips into the classroom for the impartial tasting. He's not a nice instructor. Informative, yes. Goes above and beyond to help a student out? No. Rumor has it that he once said that men make better chefs. What a jerk. I can't stand the sight of him, knowing why he's here. It will be hard to remain civil every time I have to give him a plate of my food. I shake my head and look away.

I'm not surprised that Scott's cookies are done and he's racing to put them on tasting plates. Dumbass. Always being in a hurry is going to cost him the scholarship, not the relationship between me and Taryn.

I decide on a whipped white chocolate ganache. It will make for a prettier cookie and I can dye it any color I want. I pick green to complement the pink. Perfect. My timer shrills and I race to my oven. The discs have puffed up a bit, but I know they will settle in room temperature. I pull them out, pleased with their overall appearance, and wait. If I frost them too soon, the ganache will melt and seep past the edges.

"These are good, Scott. The texture is correct and the taste is good, but you should have waited a few minutes before filling them," Taryn says. I stop and listen to them. Dr. Wright agrees with Taryn and Scott sulks back to his station. Sometimes, I can't believe he's a grown man.

Most students are finished, but I'm still waiting to frost. I match up cookie shells with like sizes and add the frosting, pleased with the results. They remind me of tulips. Perfectly pink with a hint of green. I make a dozen cookies and plate two each for each judge. I dread the walk over there. I have to act as if nothing is wrong. As if my heart isn't threatening to explode inside my chest. I have to remain calm.

"These are very good, Ki." Dr. Wright happily munches on a cookie. "The texture is great and the ganache is sweet, but not too sweet. This is white chocolate, right?" I nod my answer, my throat entirely too dry to talk. I'm two feet from Taryn and I have yet to make eye contact with her. I have no choice when she starts her evaluation.

"The cookie is light, airy, and smooth. That's the hardest part of making a macaron. Have you made macarons before?" I look at her and try my best to curb my anxiety before I speak.

"I've never made these before. They're a new favorite now."

"You did a good job." Taryn looks at me and I'm able to hold her gaze for about a second before I turn and walk away. I can feel my body shaking and I need to get out. I place my cookies in a container and label it with a single name. It doesn't take long for me to clean up my station because I didn't dirty up a lot of bowls and utensils. I'm out of there in a flash. I don't even look at Taryn. I grab my bag from the back of the class and leave quietly, happy to have a weekend where I can just be by myself and wallow in self-pity.

CHAPTER THIRTEEN

"Ki. Ki, wake up." Somebody is gently shaking my shoulder. I don't know where I am until I open my eyes and see the textured earth tone fabric of my couch. I remember showering when I got home, then crashing in the living room. I didn't even fix dinner. I grabbed Sophia and cuddled with her and fell asleep immediately. Now, somebody is waking me up from my much needed slumber, and I just want to go back to sleep. I close my eyes again. "Ki. It's me, Taryn." Now I'm awake, but too confused to move. I need to figure out why Taryn is in my house, shaking my shoulder. I roll over and stare up at her. Christ, am I dreaming? What is going on here? I struggle to sit up, but I'm too weak right now. I'll try again in a few seconds. I rub my face, desperate to wake up, or hide my emotions from her. She is in my apartment.

"What time is it? Why are you here?" I worm my way into a sitting position, careful not to touch her or allow her to touch me again.

"It's eight o'clock, and I'm here because we need to talk."

Now I'm awake. I scoot back to free myself from her nearness. "How did you get in here?" Suddenly, I'm wondering how I look. She looks great as always. Tight jeans, tight T-shirt, and sandals. I'm trying to remember what I'm wearing without being obvious. I threw on boy shorts and a tank top after my shower. I don't think I even brushed my hair so I know it must be a tangled, damp mess.

"Your door was unlocked." She sits down at the end of the couch.

"So you just came in?" I ask. She actually looks guilty.

"You left today in such a hurry, and you haven't answered my texts tonight so I had to come by to check on you."

"You didn't have to. I just didn't sleep last night and was tired," I stand up and move away from her. I need space between us. She looks me over from head to toe, not hiding the fact that she is checking me out. The tank is worthless and barely covers me, and I'm pretty sure half of my ass is hanging out of my short shorts.

"I'll be right back." I head to the bathroom to see how I look. My hair is wavy and tangled, but not as bad as I thought. I splash some cold water on my face and quickly brush my teeth. I exchange my tank for a T-shirt, hoping it offers more coverage than the tank. Satisfied that I don't look trampy, I return to the living room.

"I've never seen you with your hair down before," Taryn says. "It's nice."

"Long hair and cooking don't mix. I wear it up whenever I'm in a kitchen. People get a little upset when they find a hair in their food." I don't know why she's making small talk. "Do you want anything to drink?" I'm not really being hospitable. I just need a glass of wine to calm my nerves. I find a bottle of red and open it. I pour myself a glass and take a quick, private moment to appreciate the first sip. It's a wine with hints of chocolate and cherries. A girly wine, but one that makes my palate happy. I need happy right now. I pour a glass and hand it to her.

"Thank you for the cookies for Olivia. She squealed with delight. Pink is her favorite color, but you already know that." She takes a quick sip of wine and damn it, once again I'm focusing on her mouth. I walk back to the kitchen, glad for distance. I feel like a caged animal. Trapped, angry, sad. "Please sit down with me. I really want to talk."

"I got your message loud and clear last night, Taryn. I'm sorry I did what I did and that it made you feel uncomfortable. I don't know what else to say." I'm getting frustrated at her for making me relive a horrible moment that I want to erase from my head and my heart.

"Well, then maybe you can just listen to me." She rises from the couch and heads to the kitchen. She is graceful and confident and I'm able to keep eye contact with her until she reaches the opposite side of the kitchen island. I'm thankful it is between us, even though I have nowhere to go. I'll have to walk around her to get out. That doesn't seem like a good idea. "I'm really sorry I didn't react last night. Truly, I am. I was in complete shock. Plus Olivia was there and I didn't want to wake her. You have to understand. Olivia is everything to me. I have one shot to do what I love and have a normal life with her. Teaching is the only thing I can do that won't disrupt her life. If I lose this job, I would probably have to move and try to find another school to teach at, or screw up Olivia's schedule and go work at a restaurant again. I can't do that to her. No matter what I'm feeling or what I want. She comes first."

"Of course she does. I understand that. I actually admire you for making the choices you've made so far for both of you." I finish off my glass and pour another. I'm not a drinker, but I'm on my last nerve over here. "Most parents are selfish and won't adjust their lives for their children. You don't need to explain this to me."

"You shouldn't drink so quickly. Have you eaten dinner?" I shake my head. "The wine will make you sick." I take a long sip of it and stare at her over the rim of my glass. At this point, I don't care.

"I don't have to be anywhere," I say. I almost roll my eyes at my own immaturity. Apparently I'm going to have this temper tantrum whether I want to or not. She gives me a look. "Fine, I'll make a sandwich."

"Right now? You're going to make a sandwich right now?" She sounds exasperated.

"What do you want me to do? Listen, talk, eat? I'm confused."

My front door opens and Jessie walks in, her eyes focused on the living room, trying to seek me out.

"Why are you being so loud?" she yells. "I can hear you all the way down the hall." She freezes when she spots us in the kitchen. Her eyes widen in surprise.

"Not now, Jess," I say. She slow motion backs up until she reaches the door.

"And, I'm out." She closes the door carefully.

Any other time I would smile at her humorous attempts at cheering me up, but I'm so pissed right now at myself, the situation, at Taryn. "Christ, does anybody knock anymore?" I throw my hands up in frustration and turn back to the refrigerator. I dig around until I find turkey, cheese, lettuce, tomato, and mayonnaise. Taryn doesn't say anything, just watches me. I feel like throwing something. "Do you want a sandwich, too?" She smiles at me.

"I'd love one. I didn't get to eat dinner. My neighbor's granddaughter is over this weekend and asked if Olivia can sleepover. They are cute friends. I wanted to make sure she actually ate dinner before being pumped full of chocolate and sugar. She wanted macaroni and cheese and it just didn't seem appealing to me."

"Well, a turkey and cheese sandwich isn't much better." I toast the bread and slice the tomatoes thin. It doesn't take long to fix the sandwiches. Sophia creeps into the kitchen and sniffs at Taryn before jumping up into her lap and curling up on her.

"She's such a lover," Taryn says. And now it's awkward again. I pretend not to hear her and we eat our sandwiches in silence. My anger is dissipating. I'm just tired. I'm tired of this friction between us, drained of the unrequited feelings that eat away at my heart. I just want to curl up and hide from my emotions.

"Can we just pretend last night didn't happen?" I ask.

"No, I'm here because it did."

"So what happens now? Where do we go from here?" I'm exhausted.

"Last night's kiss was incredible. I'm not denying that we have a strong attraction." Her confession empowers me. "I'm not entirely sure what to do since I've never been in this situation before." I take her hesitancy and run with it.

"So then let's not think about it and just have the month. Let's just see what happens. This doesn't have to be complicated. Olivia already knows me and is comfortable with me." Taryn looks at me warily. "Or I can stay away from her."

"No, she really does like you. I'm not worried about that."

"What are you worried about?"

"For one, I'm pretty sure it's frowned upon at the academy. I don't know of any institution that allows teachers and students to date. And I just think we are on different levels of what we want right now. You might be running off to Italy in a month, and I want something stable. I don't get the luxury of acting on my impulses anymore." I'm still processing the fact that she wants me, and I'm not about to let her slip away. "I really have to worry about my job. I can't risk everything because of a night or two of passion."

"Or twelve or twenty."

We smile at one another. She thinks I'm kidding. I have a semester of sexual frustration and fantasies that I'm anxious to unleash with her. She leans her head back on my couch and closes her eyes. I study her, eager to reach out for her, make her mine. Instead, I wait. Everything is riding on what happens in the next ten seconds.

I watch her swallow, her neck arched, her skin smooth and pale. She opens her eyes and looks at me. It's a look of surrender. I don't hesitate. I pull her to me, closing our distance. This kiss is different. This time, I can feel the passion flow from her. Her mouth is warm and delicious, her tongue greedy against mine.

I pull her on top of me and we both moan as she stretches out between my legs. Her hips press into me, her rough jeans create friction in my sweet spot. I move my hips into her, wanting more, needing more. Her hands are already under my shirt, moving up over my ribs, stopping just short of my breasts. She's going to have to stop kissing me to get my shirt off, and right now, that's not happening.

I wrap my leg around hers, trapping her against me. I don't want her to think about what's happening right now. I just want her to act on her impulses and continue this delicious seduction. Her hair surrounds us and I dig my hands into its softness. I pull her closer into me. Her moans are deep and sensual and I can feel myself getting lost in her. I need to taste her. I want her naked. I need us to be on the bed, not squished down on my not-so-comfortable couch. She unbuttons her jeans. When her knuckles accidentally brush against my clit, I break the kiss to cry out. I'm so ready to come just from kissing. She looks down at me, her full, swollen mouth slowly curving into a crooked smile. I break eye contact only to watch her push her jeans down. She leans back to kick them the rest of the way off. Her panties are black and sexy and I smile, thinking she wore those for me. There was the possibility of this happening even before she showed up. Without hesitation, she removes her T-shirt, and before I even get a chance to admire her slim body, she crawls back on top of me. I hold her close. Our lips fit perfectly together. She grinds her hips into me and I can feel myself getting wetter just from her heat and aggression. I need to spread out and this couch is hindering my movements.

"Wait, wait." I manage to pull away for a brief second. "Let's go to my room." She licks her lips and stares at mine. I reach up and tuck her hair behind her ears before kissing her swiftly. "There's no room on the couch."

She nods and leans back so I can slip out from beneath her. My legs are wobbly when I stand up, and I don't even care that she sees how much she affects me. I reach out for her. She slips her hand into mine, and follows me to the bedroom. I can sense her nearness just from her heat. We barely make it to the bed before she crashes into me.

At least now, I can touch her everywhere. She slides down my body until she is off the bed and on her knees in front of me. For a moment, I'm confused until I feel her hands run up my thighs and reach the waistband of my shorts. I don't hesitate and lift my hips up so she can slip them off. I feel a little exposed, but my shyness is quickly replaced by need when I feel her lips trailing all the way from my knee to my inner thigh. I spread myself wider with greed and scoot closer to her warm, wet mouth. I can feel her smile against my skin. But I forget everything the moment her tongue brushes my clit. I moan. Her hands grab the inside of my thighs and spread me even wider. I'm not going to last long at this delicious onslaught. She runs her tongue softly up and down my folds, and I can't help but lift my hips and try to get closer to her mouth.

"We have all night," she says.

I know she is trying to calm me down, but I don't care. This might be our only night and I'm going to take as much of her as I can. She might be the type to regret it in the morning and never talk to me again because guilt is eating her up. No, I'm going to pretend tonight is our one and only night and find pleasure every possible moment. I mumble something incoherent, but I'm too far into this moment to actually make sense.

Much to my disappointment, her mouth leaves my body and she crawls back up to me. I lean into her when her lips find mine. I can taste myself on her tongue, which fuels my inner fire for more. I roll her onto her back and straddle her, sliding her arms up over her head. Damn, she's beautiful. I lean down and softly kiss the side of her neck. She smells like vanilla and tastes sweet and slightly salty. I nip at her earlobe and feel her rock against me. Apparently, I have found one of her sweet spots by chance. I feel her moan against me. Her hands wiggle out of my hold. Her fingers slip under my shirt and slide up to cup my breasts. I waste no time in taking my shirt off so that I'm completely naked against her. Her lacy bra and panties feel rough against my skin. Even though she is sexy as hell in her black bra and panties, I want her naked, too. I want to feel her smooth, pale skin against mine. I stretch out across her, and slip my hand between us, stroking her stomach and hips until I reach her panties. Before I take them off, I gently run my hands over them, wanting to feel her heat and her slickness through the lace. She is deliciously wet. I gently massage her until she breaks our kiss to moan freely, passionately. She presses my hand harder against her, moving her hips up and down.

"I won't break," she says.

Apparently, she likes it a little bit rough. I reach down to not so gently strip off her panties. She smells heavenly. I push two fingers into her wet pussy as far as I can go. She cries out with pleasure and I can feel her nails digging into my back. I move slowly at first, thrusting hard and deep until she starts moving her hips against me, wanting more. I stare down at her and place tiny kisses at the corner of her mouth, my tongue teasing her lips as she breathes heavily against me. I find her swollen clit with my thumb and massage it up and down with every thrust.

"Don't stop, Ki. Please, don't stop." She explodes beautifully beneath me, crying out in pleasure. I hold her while she rides out each wave until I feel her shakes subside. "That was fantastic." Her accent is even more pronounced and I smile. Her breathing is still heavy, and she starts laughing. Eventually, she stops and holds me close. "I'm sorry, but I'm laughing because I'm happy." I kiss her hard and am surprised when her body reacts to me again so quickly. Before I have a chance to continue, she rolls on top of me. She taps her fingertip on my lips. "You have an incredible mouth. I'm looking forward to seeing what else you can do with it." Christ, when Taryn makes up her mind to do something, she's all in.

"Well, then why did you climb on top of me?" I reach up and unhook her bra, pulling it off. She kisses me hard.

"Because I want to taste you again. But all of you this time." She leans down and kisses me slowly, softly. She brushes her lips over my face, down my neck and shoulders. I tell myself to relax even though I'm shaking inside. Tonight seems like a dream. She runs her fingertips down my neck, over my breasts, and back up my side. It should tickle, but my body is so wound up that the sensation is erotic. I close my eyes and enjoy her touch. Her incredible hands that I have admired so much and the magic she creates with them, is building me up. She leans over and runs her tongue over my breast, twirling my nipple inside of her mouth. I gasp at the intimacy of it, at the nearness of her. She is not gentle, but not rough either. She is sure of herself. She is making love to me as if we have been lovers for years. I wrap my fingers into her long chestnut hair, and enjoy the silky softness as it flows down my body as she kisses, licks, and sucks a trail to the junction of my thighs. Knowing that she is in complete control of me, I surrender. Her mouth is wet and hot against my clit. She licks me greedily, and I tense up, trying not to come immediately. She slides two fingers inside of me and I grit my teeth at the intensity. She is all around me, inside of me, and I'm overwhelmed with emotions. This is supposed to be uncomplicated. Simple. She runs her free hand over my thighs. I know I'm not going to last. She's a fantastic lover. She's touching me in all the right places with the exact amount of pressure, and as much as I want to continue enjoying this, I have to give in to the pleasure. I explode. She doesn't stop and I come again. After the second orgasm, I stop her because I feel like I am one quiver away from dying. She rests her head on my thighs while my body slowly floats down from the ultimate high. My fingers weave and play with her hair as we both lie there in silence. This is a big step for us. I just hope she isn't regretting her decision.

"Are you okay?" I ask.

She runs her hands up my stomach and rests them right under my breasts. She looks up at me and smiles. "Completely okay. How about you?"

I push back an errant lock of hair from her face. "Wonderful, actually." I'm not sure how much I should open up. We both have different reasons for tonight, and as casual as I wanted it to be, I'm starting to doubt the lack of commitment I've offered. I've never felt this connected to another woman this quickly before. "Come up here."

She crawls up my body, sprinkling tiny kisses all the way. When her lips find mine, the kiss is fierce at first, but settles into a slow, deep joining, and one of us whimpers. I love the taste of myself on her mouth. It's an instant aphrodisiac. I run my hands down her sides, over her slim hips, and slip between her thighs. She moans, her raspy voice encouraging me to continue.

I break the kiss and wiggle down until my head is between her thighs. I grab her hips and bring her pussy down to my mouth. I lick everywhere, tasting her, feasting on her. Her clit is swollen and I can feel her heartbeat throb inside the thin, smooth membrane. She pushes down against me. I oblige and open my mouth wide, sucking as much of her inside as I can. I want to touch her, slip my fingers inside of her, but her hips are pressed so tightly against my mouth that there isn't any room. I know she is enjoying this and is close to coming again. Her moans are getting louder, deeper. When her legs start shaking, I keep steady, constant pressure on her clit until she orgasms. I hold her hips against me, riding each wave with her. Her wetness is all over my face, down my chin. That's a first for me. She lifts herself off me and gingerly stretches out, her entire body quivering. I discreetly wipe my chin on the comforter and stretch out next to her. She rolls into me, her head on my arm, leg curled over mine. I smile because we're barely on the bed, but too tired to care. She puts her hand on my stomach and we lie there in silence for a few minutes.

"I'm glad I came by," she says. We laugh.

"I am, too." I lift her hand to my lips and quickly kiss her fingertips. I'm tired, but I've never felt more alive. It's too soon to ask what this means for us, so I reach out and grab a corner of the covers and do my best to spread it across us. I'm not cold, but I'm feeling very exposed right now. "Do you need anything?"

"A kiss would be nice."

I oblige. I lift her chin up toward my mouth and kiss her. It's a different kind of kiss. It's softer, longer, sweeter. Before it turns emotional, I slip out of our embrace.

"I'm going to get something to drink." I need distance to think. Distance to get ahold of my swirling emotions. I find my long T-shirt and quickly slip that on before I leave the bedroom. Taryn looks at me and lifts her eyebrow.

"Sophia doesn't like to see me naked." She smiles. "And I don't think I locked the door. I would hate to stumble out there naked while Jess is camped out on my couch." I walk out of the room and nearly sag against the wall. What a crazy, emotional night. Taryn seems surprisingly calm for somebody who struggled with this decision. I'm a hot mess.

I head for the kitchen after locking the front door and grab a cold water bottle from the refrigerator. I splash cold water on my face and lean over the sink thinking about the last two hours of my life. One minute, I'm asleep on my couch, the next minute I'm in bed with my teacher having hot, steamy sex. She's the most passionate woman I've ever been with. I wonder why I've been wasting my time with younger, less experienced women. I grab a bowl of grapes, an extra bottle of water, and head back to the bedroom. Taryn has moved to the middle of the bed and is comfortably under the covers. I stumble around, lighting the candles in my room. I can feel Taryn watching me and I try my best to act like the last two hours didn't change my life. I slip into bed and curl up next to her. "Are you tired?"

"Surprisingly, no."

"What would you like to do?" I ask. I run my fingertips over her smooth neck.

"I'm sure we can come up with something." Her voice is playful. The sheet falls away from her breasts as she reaches for a grape. I can't help myself so I reach down and touch her beautiful, pink nipple. It hardens immediately. She closes her eyes for a long moment and sighs against me. I lick my thumb and rub it across her nipple until she starts making little gasping noises. "You know exactly how to touch me." I slip out of my T-shirt and pull her close to me. If this is our one and only night, I'm going to get to know her likes and dislikes before morning.

❖

I wake up with a heavy feeling on my chest. I can't move my left side. For a second, I think Sophia is sitting on me. It's time to cut back on her food. Suddenly, the night rushes back. I look down at the top of Taryn's head resting on my shoulder, her arm around my waist. I hate sleeping on my back, but right now I don't mind it so much. A sensuous, beautiful woman is in my bed, something that hasn't happened in a long time. Ever actually. I look at the clock. It's just after five a.m. After a few more rounds of getting to know one another, we finally fell asleep around midnight. I'm deliciously sore everywhere. I bring a handful of her gorgeous hair up to my face and bury my nose in it. It's soft, silky, and smells like honey.

"You have an insatiable appetite." Her voice is sleepy and deep.

"Go back to sleep. I'm just touching."

"It's something I'm not used to." Her confession surprises me. I wonder about the last time she was with somebody, but I'm polite enough not to ask. It doesn't matter. This is supposed to be a day by day thing with no strings attached.

"You're too beautiful not to touch."

We both are quiet. Her breathing evens out and I know she has fallen back to sleep. I don't know what time she needs to be home, but it can't possibly be this early. I slip out from beneath her and head to the kitchen. I'm almost always up this early. I usually have to be at the diner at six, but not today.

Under normal sleepover situations, I cook breakfast in bed. I'm completely intimidated cooking for Taryn, especially given our circumstances. I pray that the grocery elves have secretly stocked my refrigerator, but after perusing its contents, I'm crushed to find so little available. I can make an omelet with mushrooms and cheese. I have grapes and watermelon and coffee. In all fairness, it's not as if I knew she was going to be spending the night. I'm just going to have to do the best I can under these circumstances. I could make pancakes from scratch, but I'm low on vanilla and that's one of my secret ingredients. I turn on the early morning news and watch it until six, giving Taryn extra time to sleep in. When the new broadcast starts, I head back into the kitchen and quietly start making breakfast.

"Would you like some help?" Taryn asks. She's wearing the long T-shirt I wore last night. Even though it's large for her, I can still see her curves. I lean over and kiss her soundly. She seems surprised, but covers it up well.

"If you want to start the coffee, that would be great." I really want her to make the omelet, but I'm embarrassed by my lack of ingredients. "I don't have a lot of food in the house so breakfast might be scarce." She waves me off.

"I don't eat a lot for breakfast so no worries. If you want, we can just eat the fruit."

"Absolutely not. We both need protein, especially after last night, and this morning." She blushes. Now she's shy? I'm nervous that she's watching me, but I'm able to get into my zone, and I manage to whip up a fluffy omelet that I'm actually proud of. I fix us plates and we sit down at the breakfast bar to eat.

"So, how did you get the nickname Ki? I've never heard that as short for Katherine."

"It's actually my initials. My full name is Katherine Ilyssa Blake, but I've been Ki my entire life. My Irish family has too many Katies already, so my dad shortened it the day I was born."

"You look like a Katie."

"What do you mean?"

"Well, you have the thick, reddish-brown hair and full lips like all Irish lassies do." She says it with an Irish accent, and it's cute since her accent is already similar. She reaches out and pulls on my hair playfully. "It's too bad I can't see it down every day."

"How about every time I see you outside of school, I'll wear it down." This insinuates that we will have more than just last night. I can almost see her mind working. She drops her smile, but nods. I want to whoop with joy. Instead, I lean over and kiss her softly. "What happens here, stays here, Taryn. Nobody will know you were here."

"I just hope I can pull it off in school."

I pull her into a long hug. "I won't even look at you." We both know I'm lying.

"Your stares completely derail me."

"I've been staring at you since day one."

She leans back and stares into my eyes. "I know."

I smile. We finish breakfast and share cooking stories. I'm fascinated with her history. She has done so much and I'm in awe of her career. Her personal life has suffered because of her career path, and becoming a single mom.

"My relationships weren't the greatest. The last serious one I had was before Olivia," she says.

I'm completely surprised at that confession. "You haven't had sex in six years?" I can't help it.

She laughs. "No. I just haven't been in a serious relationship since then."

"So, nobody's met Olivia before?"

"Nobody I've dated."

"Is this going to be awkward then?"

"No. It's different. We were friends before this happened." She moves her finger back and forth between us.

"I'm just surprised. I mean you're beautiful, smart, and successful. The fact that you're single just blows me away."

She looks down shyly. "I'm not as perfect as you seem to think I am."

I want to snort in disbelief. She's everything I said times a thousand. "You've told me that before. What are your flaws then?"

"Everybody is different. What one person considers a flaw, might not be something bad for somebody else."

"You aren't answering the question."

Her smile is tight. "Okay, then. I'm opinionated and I'm a hot head."

"That just means you're passionate. This I know for sure." I take a deep breath as I recall everything we did last night. I can't help but lean into her for a hard kiss. Our lips are perfect together. She likes to kiss as much as I do. After regretfully pulling away, I steal a glance at the clock. It's seven thirty. "What time do you have to be home?" I ask her between long and short kisses. She still smells like sex and I need to take advantage of every minute we are given.

"By ten." I pull her even closer to me. "But I also need time to get cleaned up."

"We can shower together. That will save time."

She smiles before kissing me. "Let's go back to bed." She pulls me off the barstool and playfully drags me back to the bed. I don't hesitate at all.

CHAPTER FOURTEEN

I know Taryn is going to be here. Not only is it a beautiful day, but last night we texted for a few hours and she told me her plans for the day. I just need to casually walk around the market until I run into her. It's Sunday so the River Plaza isn't as busy. Not my favorite day to shop because everything's been picked through, but I'm sure I'll find something.

"Hi, Ki," I turn to find Mary digging through the plums. Shit. Now she's going to see me, Taryn, and Olivia together like Scott did. If they show up.

"Mary, hi." I give her a small wave and walk over to her. "What are you finding?"

"Plums are in season so I'm going to make German plum cake."

"I'm sure it will be delicious." I mean it. She never disappoints. We walk down the aisle picking up fruits and vegetables and talking about the semester.

"So let me show you something." She points to the end of the market and I follow her, my curiosity piqued. We walk past a few restaurants and stop in front of a stand-alone building. It was once a restaurant, but it's empty now. "This is what I'm going to do after graduation."

I look at her until it sinks in. "You're going to open a restaurant?" I'm completely surprised and totally impressed.

"Well, more of a café, but yes. I think my pastries will be a nice addition to the market. There are very few upscale cafés in town. I believe mine will be new and refreshing."

I nod in agreement. "What a great idea." Mary went through the same change of heart career path I did, leaving nursing behind instead of law. We are about the same age, too, which makes her idea even more impressive. "I'm so excited for you."

"I know I won't win the scholarship." She holds up her hand as I object. "I just hope you win and Scott doesn't. I'm pulling for you."

"That means a lot. Thank you," I say. She really is a sweet woman.

"He's such a jerk. Yeah, he can cook well, but he's just not likable."

"Most successful chefs are jerks so he will fit right in," I say.

She laughs. "Look over there. Isn't that Taryn?" We're close to the petting zoo. My heart races when I see Taryn talking to Olivia. "Let's go say hi." Mary pulls me over to them.

"Hi, Taryn," Mary says.

Taryn turns and looks at us in surprise. "Ladies, good morning." Her voice is rich and deep and I get chills remembering that same voice whispering in my ear, encouraging me to touch her, kiss her, make her come. I try to look only semi-interested, but when we make eye contact, I can't help but feel giddy, and I can't hide the huge smile on my face.

"Is that your daughter? Oh, she's so cute. She looks just like you," Mary says.

Olivia looks up from the baby goats and waves at us. I know she's waving at me, but it looks like she's waving at all of us so there isn't any confusion on Mary's part.

"Olivia, come over here and say hello," Taryn says. Reluctantly, and perhaps because she is out of pellets, she skips over to us.

"Hello. Mum, can I please have another quarter so I can buy more food?" I'm so thankful she doesn't make a big deal out of seeing me again, only because I don't want Mary to question it.

"You have an adorable accent, too," Mary says.

Olivia looks at her like she's crazy. "Um, thank you?" We all laugh. She grabs the quarters, delighted to have two, and races off to the machine. The goats are already swarming her before she has a chance to even slip the quarters into the slot.

"I didn't know you have a daughter," Mary says.

Taryn shrugs. "I have photos of her in my office, but most students don't visit me there." An office is news to me, but makes sense. Thankfully, Mary is chatty and talks to Taryn about plum cake and other desserts she has in mind.

We won't be cooking in school much this week because Taryn has us working food prep at two different restaurants. One is Murphy's Steakhouse and the other is Atlantis, a popular seafood restaurant. I'm excited for both. Monday's class will be a quick review on cooking the perfect steak, Tuesday night will be cooking at Murphy's, Wednesday is seafood review, and Thursday night is Atlantis. We have Friday off. Taryn wants to give us the day because we have to adjust our schedules to work late at the restaurants. It's a nice reward, but I know the truth. Her mother is coming into town for a month long visit from South Africa on Friday, and she wants to be able to pick her up at the airport and spend the afternoon with her.

"Well, I need to get going. I plan to spend the rest of the day baking cakes. I'll see you both tomorrow," Mary says. I watch her walk away until I'm certain she is out of earshot.

"You look great."

Taryn looks completely relaxed and happy. Sex agrees with her. "So do you." She gives me a smile that almost stops my heart. It's a mixture of satisfaction and playfulness. It takes so much self-control not to reach out and pull her close to me. "I love your hair down."

"Ki. Hey, Ki. Look at this baby," Olivia says. The spell is momentarily broken as our attention is drawn to Olivia who has managed to pick up the smallest goat, much to the owner's chagrin.

"Honey, put the baby down. We don't want to upset her mama," Taryn says. Olivia gently lowers her until the baby squirms and leaps out of her arms, landing safely in the hay. "Don't pick up the babies, okay?" I think everybody is impressed with the fact that she was able to pick up the kid in the first place.

"You are going to have to get her a pet, you know that, right?"

Taryn sighs. "I'm hoping she'll be okay with a hamster, but I'll probably have to get her something more interactive so that she doesn't lose interest."

"Cats are great. I'm sure there are plenty at the shelter. A kitten might just be what she needs. Low maintenance, high play performance. A cat like Sophia."

"You just never know what you are going to get with a cat. As a kitten they might be perfectly sweet, but grow into a heathen."

"You say it like you have had experience," I say.

She laughs. "My best friend growing up had a sweet kitty that turned. Hit puberty and, bam, instant crazy."

"Not all kitties turn crazy. Sophia was so much fun as a kitten and just as much fun with just as much personality as an adult cat. Maybe get her two kitties so they can play together."

She rolls her eyes. "I thought you liked me."

"Oh, I like you very much." We might be crossing a line here. I'm itching to touch her, someway, somehow. I haven't stopped thinking about our night since she left. Before it gets serious, I try to change the tone of this conversation. "You should introduce Olivia to Sophia just to see what they are like together."

She nods. "Good idea. Can we wait a month? Until school is over?"

"I don't think that's up to me. It's more up to Olivia. Do you think she can wait?"

"With Grandma coming into town on Friday, I don't think she will care about a pet for several weeks. My mother will spoil her rotten until she leaves."

"I bet you're excited your mom is coming, too," I say.

"It's nice to have family close. Plus, she can watch Olivia if I want to get away for a night or two." She looks at me slyly and my heart skips several beats.

"I already like your mother. A lot. Okay, I'd better leave just in case somebody else sees us. Thank you for a wonderful weekend."

"Entirely my pleasure, Ki."

CHAPTER FIFTEEN

R emember, high heat for thin steaks, low and steady for thick," Taryn says.

We're all working the grill, testing our skills, getting ready for tomorrow night. I'm almost dancing, I'm so excited. I love the hustle and bustle of a busy restaurant. Murphy's is known for long lines every night. People will wait two hours just to eat there. I know the kitchen will be insane.

Steaks are funny. At home, people will eat whatever they cook. If they want medium and get medium well, they will eat it. At a restaurant, if they get medium well after ordering medium, they act as if a crime has been committed. I like plain steaks. A thin quick rub with olive oil, then salt and pepper and throw it on the grill. Letting it rest is probably the most important part. Patience. I know that Scott is going to have a complete meltdown tomorrow and I'm going to sit back and watch it happen.

Since we already know how to grill steaks, today is more of a refresher. When to cut fat, when not to. How long to let the steaks rest, before and after the grill, and how long to cook each cut of meat. Rib eye, T-Bone, filet mignon all have different cooking times based on thickness. Taryn is just showing us what we already know. She doesn't want us to embarrass ourselves or the institution.

I'm going to have to ask how she managed to get us this gig. Only eight of us are actually in the school's kitchen tonight. The other four are at the restaurant now working with management and will be all week. They are getting their emphasis in management, not food preparation. Eight cooks are going to be a tight fit though.

"Chef, how are eight of us, plus the regular staff, going to fit in the kitchen?" I ask.

Keeping it completely professional, Taryn responds quickly. "Executive Chef, Randy Tallis, will actually split you into two groups. First group will cook from four thirty until seven, second group will cook from seven until nine thirty."

"So why do we all have to be there at three?" Scott asks. He's already whining. Taryn looks annoyed.

"So you can experience everything about the restaurant. For those who are not cooking, you will be food runners. I will split the group up before you leave so that you'll know before tomorrow."

"Most of us already work or have worked at nice restaurants," Scott says. He just keeps digging himself deeper.

"Well, then you should be perfect at it and shouldn't have any problems," she says. I can tell by the stress in her voice that she's about ready to slap the shit out of him. He heads back to his station, grumbling the whole time. I snicker. Yep, he's going to sink.

"Why is he so upset?" Mary asks.

I shrug at her. "Maybe he really doesn't have to do a lot at his parents' restaurant and he knows that he's going to suck at it. How do you feel about tomorrow? Are you ready?" I know she struggles with proteins and I think it would be a great idea for both of us to kick his ass.

"Eh, I guess so. I'm nervous though. It's just going to be so crazy. I'm not great at cooking meats."

"Just remember to set the cut of meat out ahead of time and to let it rest after you cook it. Ten bucks says Wonder Boy over there forgets."

"I'm going to screw up the times," she says.

"Why don't you put together a list of times for the different steaks and just have it in your pocket? It will get crazy tomorrow. Or maybe we'll get lucky and be on the same shift and I can help you out." I don't want Mary upset with me, too. "But only if you want. That way you can help me with the desserts."

"That would be great, Ki. Let's hope it happens." She crosses her fingers and heads back to her station. Now, I'm even more determined to have a better night than Scott.

"How's it going over here?" Taryn is making her rounds and starts with me. I'm trying not to reach out to her. I think she knows because she's keeping her distance, too.

"Great. I think I'm teaching this filet a lesson."

She smiles at me. "Any preference?" Her voice is low and sends shivers down my spine. I lift an eyebrow at her. "Any shift preference on what time you want to cook tomorrow?"

"Later and with Mary," I whisper.

She nods her approval. "Okay, I'll keep that in mind."

It takes all of my energy not to watch her walk away. I cook the filet and the T-bone to my liking and am done quickly. I've prepared the filet medium, and the T-bone medium rare. Not my favorite way to eat steak, but they seem to be the most popular. After tasting both, I smile at the flavor. I just hope that I can cook like this tomorrow night. We've been given a menu with the recipes ahead of time and can spend the rest of class working on different items. I decide to work on their mushroom risotto. Risotto can be tricky. I've been known to add too much wine to dishes so I need to get this recipe right. After gathering all the ingredients, I heat up my skillet and thinly slice the mushrooms.

The recipe is unclear if the mushrooms are sliced or diced. I slice because I think risotto needs more shapes. It's already small. Why not add bigger things? I heat shallots and olive oil in another skillet and add the rice. Once the rice turns pale gold, I add white wine. This is the part that always confuses me. I always want to add salt. So many chefs under-salt food. After scrutinizing the recipe, I realize that the parmesan might just add the salt that is needed. I have to remind myself that I'm still a student and these chefs have years of experience. They are going to know just a tad bit more about cooking and taste than I do. My ego sometimes has a hard time recognizing that.

"Whatever you're cooking, it smells terrific," Mary says.

"Well, the ingredients aren't blended yet, but I'm hopeful."

"I for sure want to cook with you tomorrow. You have to let me taste it when it's done."

"Are you going to try anything on the menu?" I wonder if I'm the only ambitious one. I think most of the students are going to sit back and wait to be told what to do. I plan on being sous-chef. There are very few opportunities in our field to get ahead right off the bat so I plan on taking full advantage. I'll have to tell myself to not be cocky.

"I think just getting the steak perfect is enough of an accomplishment," Mary says.

I nudge her. "You have to be confident. Once you get through dinner, the desserts will be a breeze for you. That's the part I struggle with."

"All the more reason for us to pair up."

Taryn heads for the dry erase board. She's divided us up already and I'm anxious to see where she's put us on the schedule. The early shift is Scott, Brian, Lu and Josie. I'm working the second shift with Mary, Mindy and Tony. Mary and I high five. I try to contain my excitement, but I can't. Taryn smiles at us from across the room. Scott immediately calls over the three chefs on his team to boss them around.

I had my mini celebration and now it's time to finish the risotto. I blend in the mushroom slices, butter, chives and the parmesan. It still needs a pinch of salt. I add it and let it rest. Mary heads my way, fork in hand. So does the rest of my team. Apparently, they have a lot of faith in my cooking.

"Mmm. This tastes incredible, Ki," Mary says.

Tony agrees. "This is probably better than theirs." I smile. "Hey, Chef. Come over here and try this," he calls to Taryn. She heads my way and I avoid eye contact. I can't even watch her take a bite.

"Oh, Ki, you will have no problem tomorrow night. This is delicious." Taryn grabs another fork for another bite.

"Thank you, Chef." I'm finally able to look her in the eye. Pure satisfaction. She nods at me and walks back to her desk. Her control is astounding. I'm on such a high right now. Cooking really is an aphrodisiac. It's all about the senses. How does it smell? Does it look good? Does the food sizzle and pop? Is it hot enough? How does it taste? It's no wonder I want to have sex after cooking a great meal. All of my senses are on full alert.

I'm trying to figure out a way to see Taryn tonight, but I know that can't happen. Friday night was incredible, but having her only makes me want her more. For as casual as I want this to be, I find myself thinking about her constantly.

CHAPTER SIXTEEN

Everything about Murphy's Restaurant screams money. The décor, the massive wine cellar, the local artwork. I'm already in love with this place. As calming as the restaurant is, the kitchen is anything but. It's thirty minutes before service and we're learning our roles. As runners, we will carry the dishes out to the tables. This will enable us to view the plates, ensure they are hot, and compare with the order. We're to be encouraging to one another, not critical.

One of the main rules in a kitchen is don't piss off the chef. The chef indirectly affects tips, so good, hot food equals nice, fat tips. It also will bring about more business to the restaurant if people are saying, blogging, tweeting their recommendation. Murphy's is already top notch in our city. It's tough to stay on top and we really need to try our best to not give them a bad night. The Executive Chef is nervous. I don't even want to know what Taryn did or had to do to make this happen for us, but he is reminding us time and time again to check the orders, ask questions and don't screw up. I'm glad we are cooking second. It will be easier to get in the zone after having delivered plates of the food we are to make tonight.

"So, who's cooking first tonight?" the Executive Chef asks.

Scott is first to jump up and into Chef Randy's personal space. I just shake my head while others chuckle at him. He turns and scowls at us. I smile sweetly at him. I don't know where Taryn is, but I'm sure she's close by. Her reputation is on the line, too. She would cringe if she saw Scott right now. The others join in and they move to a corner to discuss the responsibility of the first shift.

I turn to the waitress I'll be following tonight, Julie, and draw her into conversation. She's very cheerful, yet not obnoxious, and knowledgeable about food. Ironically, she's working at the restaurant to put herself through law school. I don't tell her about my exact opposite decision. She loves working at Murphy's because the tips are huge and she only has to work three nights a week to live comfortably. I bet the chefs make good money here, too. Maybe if I do a great job, I can apply here and work my way up to Executive Chef sometime before I retire.

"Okay, chefs. Let's get this started," Randy says. I follow my waitress to the front of the restaurant near the bar where the waitstaff reviews specials. The chefs will cook up a plate for the entire staff to taste so they can recommend the food. Tonight's special is parmesan encrusted tilapia with wild rice and spiced carrots. I'm anxious to try Chef Randy's cooking. We review wines and what proteins they pair best with. Technically, we aren't going to recommend, but it's still important to know so I am hanging onto every word. The others in my group aren't as focused, but still respectful. I'll have to thank Taryn for putting me with the right students. I'm surprised when two plates of food are delivered for us to try. It's amazing how fast twenty minutes passes when you're learning. Chef Randy doesn't disappoint at all. The fish is flaky with just the right amount of seasoning. The carrots are spiced with thyme and sage and a sweetness I can't identify. This opens up a whole new way to eat a vegetable I'm not particularly fond of.

"Good luck today. Let me know if I can help you with anything." Randy heads into the kitchen with four Kirkwood Academy students in tow.

"Is he always this nice?" I ask.

Julie nods. "He knows that we are all part of the greater good here. If we fail, he fails. So he makes sure we don't fail."

"He's smart. A lot of chefs are idiots." She laughs. Wait until she meets Scott. I hope he tails her. She's a no-nonsense kind of girl and will definitely put him in his place.

It amazes me how early people will eat dinner. I guess they're trying to beat the crowd and get a good steak. The restaurant is buzzing, and it's just now five thirty. I shadow Julie as she takes orders, impressed with her efficiency and memory. She's very good at explaining the menu, and sold several specials already. We head into the kitchen to pick up orders. I look over the plates, pleased with what I see, and help Julie run them out to the table. The rhythm of the kitchen is building up. Sometimes, I feel like I'm in the way as we weave in and out of other runners, waitstaff, and bus boys. I haven't spent a lot of time in the kitchen observing though. I've been too busy running plates. The first break we have, I head back to the kitchen. I see other chefs at the grill, but Scott and Randy are not at the helm.

"Hey, Brian. Where's Scott?" I ask. Brian shrugs his shoulders and points his tongs somewhere behind him. I head back toward the offices and see Scott, Randy, and Taryn in the hall. Scott's face is bright red and Taryn is doing her best to calm him down. I sneak back to the grills and see Mary waiting on plates by the pick-up counter.

"Do you know what's going on with Scott?" I ask.

"Yeah, almost everything he's grilled has been sent back."

A part of me wants to throw my head back and laugh, but the professional side wins out. "What do you mean?"

"You were right. He's rushing everything. Chef Randy pulled him from the grill."

"He's better than that. I wonder why he's so freaked out?" As much as I dislike him, he does know what he's doing. Maybe he's not ready for the fast pace.

"Ki, order is up," Julie says. I grab the plates, double check the order, and send one plate back.

"Brian, this customer wanted potatoes instead of the rice on the special," I say.

"Good catch." I'm sure Julie already knew that, but wanted to make sure I caught it as well. Brian quickly replates and I'm handed the correct meal within thirty seconds. He's impressing me today. In class, he's mediocre, but in the hustle and bustle of a busy kitchen, he's killing it. As I take the plates off of the counter, I see Randy and Scott return.

Randy looks at me. "Are you Ki?"

I gulp and feel guilty for no apparent reason. "Yes, Chef."

"Deliver those plates and return here, please," he says.

I nod and quickly head out. What the hell did I do? I haven't even talked to Scott today so I don't know what it could be. I find the table, tell the patrons to enjoy their meal, and beeline it back. I find Randy at the grill.

"Yes, Chef." I feel like I'm reporting for duty.

"Will you take over Scott's position at the grill?"

"Yes, Chef." I don't hesitate. I grab my jacket, put it on, and ask Brian for an update. He is fast, on task, and a great partner at the grill. Within a few minutes, I'm grilling my first filet. I'm hovering over it, setting the timer, doing everything I possibly can to make it perfect. I flip it in four minutes and quickly get plates ready.

"Ki, what are you doing?" Mary asks. She's in to pick up an order and sees me behind the grill. Her eyes are huge.

"Chef Randy asked me to take over for Scott. I'm still going to work the second shift as long as I don't screw this up."

I'm finally getting into my zone. I pull the filet off the grill and let it rest. I'm itching to plate, but I need to show Chef Randy that I have patience and can do this right. Hell, Brian is rocking the fish so I should be able to handle this. I get the rest of the order prepped and add the filet. Brian throws together a special and we are ready to hand it over to the runners. I know the filet is perfect. No time to gloat though as a waitress hands us a five top order. Two medium T-bones, a rib eye medium well, and two specials. I get started first because the steaks will take longer. I'm able to tune everything out. It's just me and the grill. Orders come in and go out. So far nothing has come back. When it's time to switch, I stay in my chef's jacket. I'm not giving up this spot.

"Ki, are you good at this position?" Chef Randy asks.

"Yes, Chef," He nods his approval, and appoints Mary to fish. She gives my shoulder a squeeze as she passes, relieving Brian of his duty. I get a few more orders in, and get back to the grill. Scott has returned and is running food with Julie. I wink at her and she shakes her head. She's already annoyed with him. Fifteen minutes go by until I get my first return.

"Chef, the customer says the steak is too salty," Brian says. He's carrying a filet I know is perfect. I'm in complete shock. I can feel my cheeks heat up from embarrassment. I grab the plate and take a long look at it.

"It looks like the customer added too much salt. The salt on top is post heat," I say. I show Mary and she agrees.

I angrily throw another filet on the grill, pissed that a customer screwed up and blamed me. When the second steak comes back with too much salt, I'm beside myself. I'm trying to keep my cool, but I can't figure it out. What is going on out there? I throw another rib eye on the grill tempted not to even salt it at all, but I have to go with my gut and trust my skill.

Out of the corner of my eye, I see Julie and Chef Randy talking in private. This is the strangest kitchen I've ever worked in. Privacy isn't really a luxury on most days. Kitchens are small, and busy, and everybody knows everybody's business. When Taryn gets involved, I become more anxious. Again, she's angry, but she's doing a good job of controlling herself. I'm becoming alarmed. She looks over to me and motions for me to join them. Holy shit. What is going on? I ask Mary to flip my filet in three minutes and my T-bone in two. She assures me she can handle it. I head toward them.

"How many of your plates came back?" Taryn asks me. She's all teacher right now so I flip into student mode.

"Two so far, Chef."

"Why?"

"According to the customers, they had too much salt," I say.

"What do you think about that?" she asks.

"Both looked to be salted post grill so I think the customers over-salted them."

"Well, Julie just informed me that she saw Scott add salt on the way to at least one customer. She saw him drop a salt shaker into his jacket." My face heats up. "I will handle this, Chef. I just wanted to hear what you thought was going on first."

I nod. "Can I return to my grill, Chef?" I'm struggling to keep my shit together and Taryn must know because she quickly dismisses me. Don't cry, don't cry, I tell myself over and over until I get to my station.

"What's going on, Ki?" Mary asks. I shake my head. If I start talking about it, I'll cry for sure. I can't cry while I'm grilling. Chef Randy will laugh at me. Thankfully, one of the waiters turns in a four top and we both get busy at the grill. I push Scott and his sabotaging bullshit out of my head. It isn't until Brian grabs a few plates that I find out Scott is gone for the night.

"So Taryn kicked him out. Told him to go home. I wonder what happened. Do you know?" he asks us. I put a dish in front of him.

"Hey, I need rice on this plate, not potatoes." Crap. I quickly replate and hand him the corrected one. He nods his approval and slips through the doors leading to the dining room. There is a long hallway and I'm guessing Scott did the deed then. There are too many other people around for him to get away with it either in the kitchen or the dining area. What a total prick. I kind of hope he gets kicked out of the academy. I know it won't be the case, but I'm so angry right now, I'd probably throw knives at him. Really sharp, hurtful ones. And nobody would blame me.

Thankfully, the rest of the night goes smoothly. I switch over to desserts and become Mary's sous-chef, helping her with the easy stuff and even trying some of the more challenging things like Murphy's lemon mousse. By the time nine thirty rolls around, I'm ready to drop. I don't think I've ever worked this hard, this fast before. I'm on a high, but it's been dampened by Scott. I need to know what happened.

"I'm so proud of you. It's been a crazy, successful night. Thank you, Chef Randy, for allowing us the opportunity to cook in your wonderful kitchen. Students, let's clean up and get out of here," Taryn says. It only takes us about twenty minutes to clean up, and Murphy's staff actually applauds us. A few high fives and we're out the door. The air feels fresh and I don't think I've ever wanted a shower more. I can feel the grease on me. I just want to hose off and sleep for a day.

"Ki, can I see you for a minute?" Taryn asks. She still looks stressed and I want to run my hands over her face, thread my fingers through her thick, long hair and calm her down. Tonight was successful regardless of a coward's action.

"What happened?" I ask. Taryn leans against the door and sighs.

"Chef Randy had him empty his pockets and we found a salt shaker. He threw a fit and denied everything. I told him to leave. We'll deal with it at school tomorrow. Are you okay?"

I smile at her. "Of course. I almost had a no-hitter tonight. I kept up with the orders and Mary and Brian really stepped up and kicked ass in there. It was even better than I expected." She seems completely surprised by my reaction. "Look, I can't help that Scott did what he did. He's just a whiny baby and hates to lose. I can't let him get me down. You told me you would take care of it and I trust you." I almost forget we're in public and lean into her. I realize I'm entirely too close and take a step back.

"That's very gracious. And yes, it was a great night aside from that. You all did well, but I'm so proud of you for stepping up and taking over. Fantastic." I can tell she wants to touch me, but can't.

"Thank you. I can't wait to go home and crash." She walks me over to my car. "I'll see you in the morning." I crawl in and fasten my seat belt.

She leans down so that she's close, but not too close. "I wish I could show you how proud I am of you."

Suddenly, I'm awake. "If you can come over, that would make this day perfect." I want to reach out and pull her to me for a long, powerful kiss.

She looks sad. "I can't. Olivia."

I nod. "I know."

CHAPTER SEVENTEEN

"So what happened?" I'm really early to class because I'm dying to know what happened with Scott. Taryn looks up and around.

"I thought about calling you earlier, but then I remembered you were at the diner this morning. I bet you're tired." She's wearing a suit and looks incredible. The taupe jacket is hanging on the back of her chair. The skirt is tight and the blouse is fitting, but not revealing. Very tasteful and very feminine. Not that I didn't already know this, but she cleans up very well.

"I am, but I can sleep Friday." I put my bag down and actually sit at my desk. "So?"

"Well, I reported it to Dr. Wright and had a meeting with both him and Scott. Scott denied everything. He's on probation even though I pushed for a harder punishment. Dr. Wright will no longer be second guessing me now. He did say that it was the waitress' word against Scott's and I should be more supportive of the students here."

"That's it? He gets talked to and that's it?" I'm mad. I just want what was fair. "When people cheat, and I do consider this a form of cheating, most students get expelled. So because he's a man, he gets special treatment? They both are jerks." I'm pissed.

"Trust me. I fought for what I thought was right. I'm sure Dr. Wright thinks I'm picking on Scott given what happened a few weeks ago. I'll never give Scott a recommendation, and it will be hard for him to get a job here once word of mouth gets out." That doesn't make me feel any better. I can see it now, he will win the scholarship all because he's a guy. This is so unfair. I look at Taryn and I know that she tried. I can tell just from the look in her eyes. She seems sad, but determined. I soften.

"I know you did, Taryn. I trust you." I take a moment to rid myself of my shitty attitude. After a deep sigh, I put myself back into the conversation. "By the way, you look beautiful today all dressed up."

"I wanted the department to take me seriously." She smiles at me and suddenly it doesn't seem so bad. Nobody is in the class yet, so I take a private moment.

"When do I get to see you again?" My voice is low.

She looks at me and thinks for a moment. "My mother arrives Friday so I'm sure she can watch Olivia for a bit this weekend."

"Great." I smile and head to my station. I want to sit and talk with her until class begins, but we have to be careful since it seems as if the entire class is under scrutiny now. Mary shows up, and after putting on her jacket, she heads my way.

"So, what happened last night?" I don't feel bad telling her. Scott is going to look like an ass no matter who tells the story. She's in complete shock. "What a dick." She looks completely disgusted with him. "That makes zero sense. He's a good chef, so why would he cheat?"

"Well, he completely panicked. I knew he would rush and not let the steaks rest. That's why Chef Randy had me switch with him. He pulled him off the grill, put me on, and Scott had some sort of a meltdown because of it. I'm certain I got the win last night." We both laugh at that. "You and Brian did a really great job on the grill. And here you were, worried the whole time."

Mary smiles at me. "It's easy when you have somebody next to you who knows what she's doing. And Brian was great because I think he works at Applebee's and cooks steaks every day. He's had tons of practice." The diner doesn't serve a lot of steak so I learned by grilling on my deck and having Jessie, Lynn, and Sam be my guinea pigs. Steak, regardless if you work at a high end restaurant or bar and grill, is always in demand. The rest of the students file in. Not surprisingly, Scott is the last one in. He walks right over to his station, his head down, keeping to himself. I'll be surprised if he says anything to me. He's not one to lose graciously. I see Taryn look up at the clock and slip into her chef's jacket to start class.

"Why are you so dressed up today, Chef?" Brian asks.

"I had a meeting with Dr. Wright." I can still hear the anger in her voice. "Okay, let's talk about the seafood dishes you will be preparing tomorrow night." She's not going to elaborate to anyone and we all slip into student mode.

I need to pay attention today because fish is not my strongest food. I don't love it, so it's hard to get my palate right. I make a mean crab cake and can fluff up a scallop, but I suck at deboning and getting the right heat on fish. I tend to overcook it, so I really need all the help I can get before tomorrow's service. Thankfully, there are enough options that we can pick a station and stay with it all night. All eight of us will be in the kitchen at the same time so it will be almost impossible to sabotage anybody's food. Taryn lists the different stations and we get what we want. I'm on scallops and mussels, Brian's on chicken and steak, Mary gets soups and desserts, and Scott gets fresh water fish. There are other stations she assigns, but I'm not paying attention.

I'm not strong on mussels and plan to spend today's class focusing on them. Atlantis has them served several different ways; simmering in garlic butter, swimming in white wine, saffron and tomatoes, or just steamed. Most of the mussels are served with pasta, so I have to get my pastas down pat. I'd love to create a mussel ravioli, but that's not on their menu. I'm told most of their pasta comes from a box. Boring, but fast. I review their menu and get started on the mussels. The first batch comes out rubbery. I'm frustrated, but not deterred.

"What's going on here, Ki?" Taryn asks. I blow a piece of hair out of my face in frustration. I can tell she wants to reach out and tuck it behind my ear, but instead she crosses her arms in front of her and takes a step back.

"My mussels aren't cooking right. Why are they coming out like erasers?"

"You need to use a wider pot so they aren't all stacked. The bottom ones are cooking, but waiting for the upper layer to cook will make the bottom ones overcook, and become rubbery," she says. She tastes the wine sauce. "The sauce is delicious. Once you spread out your mussels, you'll be fine." I raise my eyebrow at her and she blushes.

"Um, well, okay. I guess I will get another pot and try it again." I'm looking forward to the weekend. Even if it's for only thirty minutes, I'll take it. I miss her mouth. I miss her lips on mine, her taste. I give a quick shake of my head. I can fantasize about us tonight when I'm alone in bed. After fifteen minutes of regrouping, and making a few minor adjustments, I'm able to cook the mussels perfectly. I wish I had the crab cakes station, but I'm sure the scallops and the mussels will be enough to keep me on my toes tomorrow night. After looking at the clock, I see that I have time to cook up a few scallops. I blacken them just for kicks and almost cry with joy when I taste one. It's perfect. Spicy and juicy.

"Is this even on the menu?" Taryn looks at scallops on my plate. I sheepishly shake my head no.

"I couldn't help myself. But in all fairness, I did use the recipe and cooked a few per their instructions. I thought they were kind of tasteless so I decided to add heat. Taste one." She grabs a fork and knife and gently places one on a small plate. She pokes the texture with her fork and watches the meat carefully as she cuts into it.

"They are cooked well," she says.

"Wait until you taste it." I'm excited. I watch as she slowly puts the bite into her mouth. I love that she always closes her eyes when she tastes my food. I wait five whole seconds before prodding her for a review. "And?"

"Perfect." She takes another bite and moves to the next station to talk to Brian. She looks over her shoulder and smiles at me.

"Oh, how sweet. Your girlfriend loves your food," Scott says. He is suddenly in my personal space and my warm, fuzzy feeling is instantly replaced with icy anger. Without hesitation, I turn to him.

"Too bad you have to cheat to beat me." I smile at him and bat my eyelashes. He scowls and marches off to his station. Asshole. I hope he crashes and burns again tomorrow. I clean up my station, still pissy over our encounter.

"Don't worry about him. He's acting like a jealous ass. Come on, let's get out of here," Mary says.

As much as I want to stay and be near Taryn, I'm afraid it will be obvious so I grab my bag and head out with Mary instead. By the end of class today, the rest of the students heard about what Scott did and kept to themselves. Nobody talked to him, nobody asked for assistance. I kind of love my classmates right now. Tomorrow night is going to be interesting.

❖

It's eight o'clock and I'm already in bed with Sophia. I'm exhausted. The television is on, but I'm bored. I really want to text with Taryn. I know she is busy with Olivia and getting ready for her mother's visit. I'm trying to be mature and not clingy. Reminding myself that this is supposed to be casual isn't helping either.

My phone buzzes with a text from Taryn. *Are you relaxing?*

My heart picks up speed. She must be reading my mind. *I'm already in bed. I don't think I can move.*

It's been a long week for you already.

I'm looking forward to Friday, so I can chill. As much as I want to ask about the weekend, I need to settle down. She will let me know when and if she can get away. *You're probably excited for your mum to visit.* I say "mum" like she does because I think it's adorable.

Definitely. I can't wait until they move back for good.

I miss you. I'm too tired to tiptoe around my feelings today. I realize I'm squeezing my phone, waiting for her reply. When it vibrates, I jump.

And I miss you.

I can't remember the last time I smiled this much. *Can I call you or is Olivia awake?*

My phone rings in my hands. I smile.

"I need to hear your voice," I say.

"I missed you today. You left so quickly."

"Scott was being stupid, so I left with Mary. I tried to get your attention, but you were helping Tony with crab cakes."

"What did Scott do?" she asks.

"Eh, it's not important. Let's not talk about him. He managed to ruin last night, but he's not going to ruin tonight."

"Good point and good attitude. Are you ready for tomorrow?"

"You tell me. Do you think I'm ready?" I ask.

"Without a doubt. Fantastic scallops today. Too bad you can't share your recipe with them. Yours are far better."

"Scallops are such a boring food. I don't care for seafood, so I try all sorts of things to make it taste better. Maybe I should try it with my chutney."

She laughs. "Nothing about that sounds appealing."

"How's Olivia?"

"Finally asleep. She's been wired all week. I think she's going through another growth spurt. She's irritable one moment, then excited, then tired. I can't keep up with her. Puberty is going to be the death of me."

"Tell me about the day she was born," I say.

"Um, okay." She sounds surprised, but excited to talk about it. "First of all, I was huge. I was a whale while pregnant with her."

I can't even imagine her larger than a size four. "Oh, stop. You probably only gained ten pounds."

"Oh, more like thirty pounds. I ate all of the food I cooked." I snort. Thirty pounds is average weight gain during a pregnancy. "Well, one night my back started hurting, so I called my mum and she rushed over. She could tell that I was close. I was miserable. I couldn't get comfortable. My water broke, and before I had a chance to freak out, she got me to the hospital. Labor wasn't too bad, but my hips will never be the same."

"How long were you in labor?"

"Not long actually. About six hours, which is really quick for a first baby. I'm so thankful my mum was there with me. I couldn't imagine doing that on my own."

"She's a great kid. Very polite and sweet," I say.

"I got lucky for sure."

"And by the way, your hips are perfect," I say.

She clears her throat. "Thank you. I was afraid I wouldn't be able to get any sort of figure back after Olivia was born."

"I don't know what you looked like before, but you look great now." I'm feeling all warm and fuzzy recalling our one night together. I'm desperate for the next one. "You're going to have to wear a nice suit during finals like you did today. That will be my driving force to cook the best meal I've ever cooked before."

"You will cook the best meal because of you, not because of me," she says. I sigh. "But I might wear something a little encouraging." I perk up. Her laugh is low and raspy. I can tell she's getting aroused.

"I really wish you were here."

"Soon." That's both encouraging and deflating. I'm not ready to give up. Just because we aren't together, doesn't mean we can't share an intimate moment right now over the phone.

"After you left Saturday morning, I could still smell you on my sheets and on my body. I didn't want to get out of bed." I even masturbated after she left. "What a great night."

"It really was fantastic."

"You know, if your mother is in town for several weeks, maybe we can sneak away for a whole weekend. We can leave early Saturday morning and get back Sunday night. That way you are only gone for a night." I'm excited at the possibilities.

"What would we do?"

Eat, cook, have sex. Have sex, cook, eat. The possibilities are endless. "I'm sure we could find a nice bed and breakfast, or a suite where we can cook, shop, and spend time alone." In my mind, I'm jumping up and down with glee. "Or just time alone. Let somebody else cook for us."

"That sounds really nice. I'm sure my mum can keep Olivia entertained." While she is interested, I offer to find us a place no more than three hours outside of town. Suddenly, I'm not tired anymore.

"I can look, too. I'm sure we can find something."

Preferably a room with thick walls and a staff who will leave us alone. Too bad we can't fly somewhere tropical. I would love to see Taryn in a bikini lounging by a pool. There is so much I want to do with her, and no time to do it. "When do you think?" I don't want to push, but we're running out of time. School will be over in three weeks. This weekend is out because her mom arrives. "Maybe next weekend?"

"I'm sure I can get away then. Let's plan for it," she says.

"Great. Let me grab my laptop." I search north of town because there isn't anything around, and we're not likely to run into anybody. "Oh, here's a quaint place about two hours away that boasts tons of bike trails." I give her the website so she can review the site with me.

"It looks massive. The trails look great. I haven't been on a bike ride in forever." Okay, so that's not the kind of physical activity I had in mind, but I can compromise.

"I'm sure they have bikes we can rent." My bike probably has tons of cobwebs on it. I'd rather buy a new one than go into my spider infested storage unit and clean it off.

"Let's do it. I'll go ahead and book it."

I think she's worried if I can afford it. "It's my idea. Let me."

"It will be my treat. And that's final."

"Then I'll take you to a nice dinner." I'd prefer to make her a nice dinner, but unless we stay at my apartment, that's just not going to happen. I'm pretty sure getting out of town is probably the best thing.

"I would love that."

"It would be better if I could cook for you," I say.

"You cook for me five days a week."

"That's not the same. I cook because I have to, and I'm required to cook certain things. I want to cook something that I want to cook. Something that's not on the syllabus."

"You did. You cooked me incredible salmon on the first day."

Oh, yeah. I forgot about that. "But that was in a classroom setting. Plus, salmon is about the only fish I know how to cook well."

"If you could cook me anything, what would it be? Maybe that should be the final."

"You don't know what our final is going to be yet?" I'm surprised. She laughs.

"I have an idea, but I can't share it with you." She's teasing. I wouldn't want her to tell me anyway. If I win, I want it to be fair and square. And I will win.

"Oh, I'll win. Scott doesn't stand a chance." We both fall quiet. It's been a rough week so far. I just need to get through tomorrow night. Of course, then there is the whole going off to Italy two weeks after the semester ends thing. If we keep this relationship going until then, it will come to a screeching halt in about a month. As much as I don't want to think about it, I do. Is it fair to start a relationship, regardless if we say it's going to remain casual, knowing that it could all end suddenly?

"You're quiet. What are you thinking about?"

I can't tell her because I'm not ready to give her up just yet. I want to be greedy with the time she affords me. "I guess I'm just tired." Suddenly, phone sex seems cheap. I decide to not continue down that path and instead talk to Taryn about her plans with her mom. We're on the phone for almost forty-five minutes before I squeak out a yawn that Taryn hears.

"Get some rest. You have to get up early tomorrow. Sleep well."

We hang up and I feel sad. I'm happy that we get to spend a weekend together, but down because I don't think this is going to end well.

CHAPTER EIGHTEEN

The kitchen in Atlantis is in full swing by the time I arrive. I'm the last one here and that surprises me. I'm even fifteen minutes early.

"How long have you been here?"

Mary turns to me, her face etched with concern. "Only about ten minutes. I wanted to find out if Chef Matthew is as tough as they say. The answer is yes, in case you were wondering."

We both turn and face the kitchen. As chaotic as it might seem to the untrained eye, it's very organized. There is a natural flow between chefs and the waitstaff and I'm impressed with this kitchen. I see Taryn tucked in the back corner near the station I will be cooking at. I can't help but smile. I can use a bit of her good luck. She spots us and heads our way.

"So far, the service has gone extremely well." Since all of us are here, she preps us so that we can jump in when the restaurant's chefs jump off. Taryn has us spend a few minutes with the chefs and shadow them until we relieve them.

"Good luck." The regular chef here says, handing over the tongs.

I easily slip into the zone. He has the right temperatures going and I plan to maintain them. Mary is on the other side of my grill so she can yell if she needs help. We continue the good luck streak and crank out the orders like we've worked there for years. It's a magnificent kitchen. Even though it's primarily seafood, I wouldn't mind working here after school is over. It could only help me learn how to cook seafood perfectly. Scott seems to be shining, much to my chagrin. I notice the rest of the team is not talking to him and I'm sure they are worried that he is going to do something shady to their dishes. Nobody is leaving their station. Wise decision, I think. Chef Matthew is hovering, pointing out the good and the bad. I have a feeling I'm in for a long night. We only had one steak come back. My mussels were either cooked well, or the customers didn't complain. Thankfully, not too many people ordered them. The scallops were a hit, but as a whole, we all did well. I can almost see Taryn sigh with relief as she and Chef Matthew discuss the night's events.

"That wasn't so bad. I'm sure Chef is proud of all of us," Mary says. We give a weak high five and head for the exit. The staff of Atlantis isn't as friendly as Murphy's, so we leave without applause. As a matter of fact, I don't believe Chef Matthew even said a word to me. That's okay. I kind of like being under the radar once in awhile. I'm not as tired as I was the night we cooked at Murphy's, but I'm pretty sure I need to head straight to bed.

My phone buzzes about two minutes before I'm home. I look down and see that it's a message from Taryn. I know I'm supposed to wait until I'm safely parked, but pull up the message.

Everybody did well tonight. Chef M was impressed.

I hurry up and head to the parking lot before I answer. *I noticed it was peaceful. I guess Scott didn't cheat.*

No, I stood close by him the whole night.
Did it hurt?
Lol. He behaved.
Ugh.

I sprint up the stairs to my apartment. I can't wait to shower. I smell like seafood. I quickly shower until I'm sure all of the grease is off of my body. It's amazing how dirty you get just from one night. Long sleeves and long pants protect your skin and keep you relatively clean, but your face, neck, and hair feel like you've been camping in the wild for a week. I hear my phone ding so I know Taryn has sent me another message. I towel off before I check my phone.

Can you come over?
Holy shit. *Is everything okay?*
I want to be with you.
I don't hesitate. *I'm on my way.*

I slip on the bathroom tile and bang my knee against the sink. Damn it. I hobble down the hall to my bedroom to put clothes on. I don't even bother with panties. I find some yoga pants, a tank top, and top it off with a light zip-up workout jacket. I'm sure I look like a drowned rat, but I don't even care. With minimal late night traffic, I reach her apartment in less than ten minutes. I park two blocks away. I'm not taking any chances. I put my hood up and jog to her place. Her door is ajar. I slip in and close it softly.

"You shouldn't leave your door open like that." I keep my voice low so I don't wake up Olivia.

"I just opened it. I knew you would be here soon." Taryn is wearing thin pajama pants and a matching sleeveless camisole that leaves nothing to the imagination. I lock the door before I head directly toward her, only one thing on my mind. She takes a step back before she opens her arms to me. I crash into her, pushing her up against the wall. She whimpers when we finally kiss, our mouths devouring one another. I can't get enough of her. I suck her tongue into my mouth, bite her bottom lip, but the ache is still there.

"Let's go to your room," I say.

She nods and we tiptoe to her room, closing the door behind us. We pick up where we left off with more fervor. She unzips my jacket and practically rips it off of my body. We fall onto the bed and she crawls on top of me. Her weight is wonderful against the ache between my thighs. I buck up while she pushes into me and I moan with pleasure.

"Shh, we have to be quiet," she whispers.

Shit. That's right. I look at her and nod. I reach down and tug her top off, anxious to feel her soft skin against mine. I wind my hands into her long, soft hair and bring her mouth back down to mine for a kiss. She starts grinding her pussy against my leg and I reach down to help alleviate the ache I know so well. Her pajamas are soaked. I can smell her wetness, her essence filling my senses. I need to taste her again.

I roll her over and slide down her slender body. She lifts her hips up to me and I kiss her mound through her pants before I yank them off. I dive into her, spreading her wide with my hands. We both moan the moment my tongue hits her slit. I feel her fingers weave in my hair, pulling me into her. Her hips are moving into me, her pussy grinding against my mouth. I'm breathing hard, trying to catch my breath, and make her come at the same time. She hooks the back of her knees over my shoulders and grabs the covers. I slide my hands over her stomach and up until I reach her breasts. Her nipples are hard and the second my hands cup them, she covers my hands with her own and squeezes.

It's unbelievable how sexual she is, how open she is with me after only a short time. When her knees start shaking, I know she's going to come. I wish I could be all over her, touching, tasting, riding her orgasm out with her. She grabs a pillow and covers her face as the orgasm washes over her, her moans suppressed by a cushion. I wish I could hear her, but I know that we have to be quiet, no matter what. Her juices are all over my face, but I don't care. I gently slip one, then two fingers into her still contracting pussy. Her back arches off of the bed and she makes a noise and quickly covers her mouth with her own hand. I can feel her heartbeat quiver around my fingers.

I can feel my heart slipping. I need to get a grip on this. I can't lose myself in her. She leans back on her elbows and watches me. I can't look away. As much as I want to move up and kiss her, there is something so erotic in watching the passion ignite in her eyes, her mouth open, her breasts rise and fall as her breathing increases. She hisses the deeper I move inside of her, and groans with seeming regret as I slip out. Her stomach muscles tighten as she welcomes her second orgasm. She bites her lip to keep from crying out. Christ, I can't get enough of her. I want to spend as much time as I can just watching her come. She falls back on the bed, breathing hard. I stop moving inside of her, but I'm not ready to leave her warmth. I slide up her body, placing kisses on her skin until we are face to face. She pushes my wild hair out of my face and kisses me soundly.

"Wow," she says.

I shush her. Even though she thinks she's being quiet, she's not. Her smile wavers and for a moment, I think she's going to cry. She kisses me again, covering up any emotion I think I might have seen. I lie beside her until we're both breathing normally. The second I slip out of her, I miss her warmth. Our connection is broken and I can't get close enough to her. I place tiny kisses on her face. Her lips are soft and greedy when they meet mine. I want to keep this intimacy longer. I pull her against me so that her head is resting on my shoulder. She slides one of her legs between mine and we lie there. I play with her hair as she lightly strokes the side of my neck.

"You have the softest skin," she says.

I bring her fingertips to my lips and kiss them. "I just got out of the shower. I'm a mess."

"You did a good job tonight. Chef Matthew even said so."

"He didn't say a word to me."

She smiles. "He only talks if there is a problem, so know that you did well."

"How did you manage to get these cooking gigs for us, or do I want to know?" I ask.

"Well, I worked with Chef Randy. His restaurant is one of the few who agreed to help the academy. I don't think Chef Matthew was excited for us to be there, but it wasn't his decision."

"As fun as it was, I'm glad we are done with Hell Week. This week was like starting a new job twice." She rests her palm right above my heart. I try not to read too much into it. "I want to go back to class and be done with my night by six."

"This week was hard for you because of the diner. Oh, and you have to work there in just a few hours. I'm so sorry I called. It wasn't fair of me." She doesn't know that I will drop anything for her.

"I can sleep after I'm done with my shift." I take a peek at the clock. "Plus, I can still squeeze in a few hours."

"But I'm not done." She slides over me, bringing my arms up over my head. I love that she is naked and I'm still clothed. "When I said I need you, it wasn't because I wanted you to give me two really great orgasms." I smile. "Well, don't get me wrong, I'm not going to stop you, but I need to feel you and taste you again. I couldn't wait until next weekend."

"Perhaps it was my command of the kitchen that turned you on and you just couldn't stop thinking of me." I joke, but we both know that having a perfect run in a kitchen really is some type of natural high that you want to share with someone.

"That probably had something to do with it." She leans down and kisses me. "You were amazing this week." She slides my tank up and over my head. I watch her run her fingertips lightly over my breasts and down my stomach. She lowers her head and slowly licks my nipple. I close my eyes and surrender to her mouth and her touch.

CHAPTER NINETEEN

L et's go." Jessie is standing in my living room, loudly tapping her foot, waiting for me to finish putting on my makeup. "The hot girls are all going to be taken by the time we get there." I have no desire to go out, but Jessie has been on me to be her wingman for weeks. She's always been there for me, so I can't let her down. Plus, she might get suspicious if I don't participate, and I might accidentally let it slip that I've been with Taryn. I like our secrecy.

"Give me two minutes." I quickly put on my mascara and give myself the last minute look over. I grab my shoes and head down the hall. Jessie gives me a nice whistle.

"Maybe we should hook up like your teacher thought we were doing," she says.

I playfully smack her on the arm. "Stop. Let's go."

Jessie practically skips out the door. Saturday night at the club will certainly get her laid. I'm guessing she won't even leave before that happens. Hearts Afire is a club I don't attend a lot. It's more of a warehouse where a lot of women dance, drink, do drugs, and have sex. I'm guilty of three of the four. I don't do drugs. We get into Jessie's Jeep and drive the fifteen minutes to the club. She's brimming with excitement. I'm dreading it. I want to be invisible tonight. Even though Taryn and I talked about keeping our secret relationship casual, every time I'm with her, I care for her a little more.

"I hope we have some fresh meat tonight," Jessie says.

I roll my eyes at her and she just laughs. "You are such a pig."

"Don't knock it. When was the last time you got laid? It's been a long time."

Less than forty-eight hours, but I'm not sharing. "Sometimes it's not just about sex. Sometimes it's about a relationship."

"You definitely need to get laid," she says. I roll my eyes again.

We find parking close to the club and head inside. I avoid all eye contact even though Jessie is talking to everybody she sees. I'm just not in the mood. We make our way to the bar and order beers.

"Look at that girl down at the end of the bar," Jessie says. I see a cute blonde looking over at us, even though she's surrounded by friends. Jessie tips her beer at her and smiles. The girl comes over to us.

"I haven't seen you two in here before. My name's Nikki."

"I'm Jess and this is Ki," Jessie says.

"Ki. What a cool name."

Even though she's cute, I don't want to talk to her. I mean, maybe if things were different for me, then I would. She keeps trying to draw me into conversation. Jessie picks up on it and leaves, winking at me. Now I'm stuck. Nikki is a physician's assistant, five years older than me, and lives downtown, a few blocks from the club. She flags the bartender over for two more beers and a couple of shots. She gives her a credit card before I can argue.

"I can get my own drinks." I know she's being nice, but she's not getting into my pants, or up my skirt.

"It's my pleasure." She leans in closer to hear me better. The club is getting louder and talking is even proving difficult. "Hey, finish your beer and we'll hit the dance floor." I finish my beer in two long swallows. She grabs my hand and we find a relatively free spot. The beat is fast and fun and we start dancing. It's awkward at first until we find a comfortable rhythm together. I should be having fun, but all I can think about is Taryn. I see Jessie on the other side of the bar kissing a leggy brunette. It's just a matter of time before she has her in a dark corner or in the bathroom.

Nikki leans in. "Let's grab another drink." She grabs my hand before I can respond and we head back to the bar. She orders more shots. I don't really want to drink any more, but I take the tiny glass and toast with her. "Here's to new friends." We clink glasses and gulp down the alcohol. I give a little shiver when I'm done and she laughs at me. "Do you want to get out of here?" We both know what that means. Her hand is on my knee.

"I can't, but thanks for the offer."

She leans in and kisses me. It doesn't feel like it's supposed to. It doesn't feel like anything. Her lips are nice, and she tastes sweet, but there is no fire. Apparently, I can't do casual. She breaks the kiss and stares at me before tossing back the rest of her drink.

"So tell me about her," Nikki says.

"Not much to tell really. We're new and trying to figure things out."

She nods. "I've been there and done that. Here, give me your phone." I hand it to her and she adds her number. "Call me if you ever want to talk or dance." I can't help but smile. Two months ago, I'd already be at her place, but now I'm just not feeling it.

"Thanks, Nikki. I might just do that."

She winks and leaves. I look around. I can't find Jessie anywhere. I order another beer, sit back and wait for her to show up. The music is loud and right up my alley.

"Let's dance." Jessie hugs me from behind, spilling my beer. She kisses my cheek and drags me off of my stool and onto the dance floor.

"So what happened to legs?" I ask. It's more like a scream because she can't hear my normal voice. Jessie winks at me. I shake my head at her. She laughs. We dance for about thirty minutes. I'm hot and tired and Jess even looks like she's had enough action. We grab one another and head to the bar for cold waters.

"Thanks for coming out with me. I know you've been worried about school, and I was hoping that you would forget about everything for at least one night."

"I'm hanging in there. Thanks for inviting me. I did meet Nikki." I don't tell her that Nikki will only ever be a friend.

"Okay, don't hate me, but let's go home," she says.

I don't hesitate. I finish my water and grab her hand. "I'm ready." We weave through the dancing women, and take a deep breath when we finally leave the club.

"I still had fun even though we didn't stay long," she says.

"Are you going to call legs or was that it?" I ask.

"It was fun, but that was probably it."

"So do you ever want a real relationship?"

"What do you mean?"

"Well, for one, you have sex with the same person, and only that person more than once. And you talk every day, make decisions together, have meals, and plan trips. You laugh and cry together, and support one another." I could go on, but she interrupts me.

"How many of those have you had?"

"Yeah, I know, but that's what I want now." I'm tired of this scene. I'm tired of the unemotional sex and the crazy women.

"So are you thinking about Taryn?"

"That would be nice."

"Even though she has a kid?" I give her a look. "An adorable kid, but still, a kid? Isn't she really an untouchable? Single mother with child? Are you really ready for that?" She's got me there. I've been so focused on Taryn and sex with her, I haven't really thought about Olivia and what that will do to her. Taryn and I kind of talked about it, but without resolution. We're keeping it light because there is a good chance that I will be gone for ten months. "Plus, you'll be in Italy for almost a year. Italy with beautiful women who are fantastic lovers."

"How do you know that?"

She winks at me. I just laugh. She's completely hopeless and I'm completely hopeful.

CHAPTER TWENTY

"We only have two more weeks left of class, chefs. Let's keep it together and try to get through the German lesson," Taryn says.

I'm the only one who is excited about making German food. Ever since the Ethnic Food Festival, I've been itching to try that nice lady's sauerbraten recipe. It's all about the sauce. The cuts of meat are different and I'm pleased with what Taryn has available for us. We have roasts, topside beef, veal, and turkey cutlets. She has shown us the proper way to cut the meats for popular German dishes including schnitzel, rouladen, and sauerbraten. Yesterday she even showed us how to make spaetzle, a rough texture noodle that is served with the proteins we're learning how to master. My sauerbraten has been marinating twenty-four hours and I'm anxious to start my sauce.

Two of us are trying sauerbraten; Brian is making rouladen, and the rest of the class is making schnitzel, including Scott. That's about as difficult as cooking a pork chop. I grab my ingredients, close my eyes, and get into my zone. Today, I plug in my headset and listen to music. I've been obsessing about my upcoming weekend with Taryn. If I listen to loud music, I can't recall the last night we spent together. My memories of fucking her, tasting her, making her come again and again is repressed by the loud music.

I don't think about her unless I catch her out of the corner of my eye helping a student or working on her laptop. When she looks at me, my knees get weak. I'm not going to survive. I'm going to have to see her before our weekend. The other night was incredible. I only slept an hour. Her appetite is insatiable. When I finally fell asleep, I woke up to her behind me, sucking on my neck and her fingers deep inside of me. I came fiercely, quietly, remembering not to wake up Olivia down the hall. I climbed up the headboard as she drew out another orgasm. What a fantastic way to wake up. Since her mother is in town now, I can't just sneak over there. She'll have to come over to my place, but I have a feeling she'll wait until the weekend. I shake off my memories and focus on my sauce. It's sour enough and I scoop out a cup to add the gingersnap crumbs. Much to my delight, it really does enhance the flavors. I add some to the rest of the sauce.

"How does it taste?" Taryn is suddenly beside me. I take out my earbud. The urge to dip my finger in the sauce and let her lick it off is great. My lust must be showing because she takes a step back. I look down quickly so that nobody can see me and I take a deep breath. She finds a spoon and quickly takes a taste. "This is really good." She puts her spoon in the sink and heads to Mary's station without looking back at me. Shit. I really need to leave my hunger for her at the door. I'm going to have to apologize to her later. "Be sure to prepare several small plates for your colleagues," she says.

I opted not to make the noodles, and make mashed potatoes instead. The gravy will be better served with potatoes. Everybody else is making spaetzle and I second guess myself. Apparently, I'm not the only one.

"Why did you decide on potatoes?" Mary asks.

"Don't tell Chef, but I really don't like the texture of them. I guess I'm Americanizing the dish. Mashed potatoes are the perfect pillow for this gravy," I say.

Mary grabs a spoon and tastes the sauce. "This is good. I think you're right. The mashed potatoes will enhance the gravy. Good call."

While the beef rests, I start mashing my potatoes. Such a comfort food. I might have to make this my dinner tonight. It's five now so I have another hour until we have to be out of here. Most people are done. The three of us who picked the harder meals are standing around making sides while our proteins cook. I opt for a cold red cabbage salad that will add texture and acid to my plate. At this point, I'm cooking for Taryn. By five thirty, I have four plates ready to serve. I serve Taryn first, then leave the plates for Mary and Brian, the only ones still in the classroom. I head back to my kitchen to finish mine.

I don't even wait for their reviews. With only four of us in the kitchen, they can talk to me from across the room and I will hear them. I taste my own food as though it's somebody else's. I have no complaints. The meat is tender, juicy and the creamy potatoes help dull the sour sauce. The salad provides a nice crisp to the meal. I start cleaning up my station, taking bites of my dinner in between running dishes to the washer. By the time I'm done, Taryn and I are the only ones left in the room.

"You impressed me," she says. She walks over to me and I don't even hide that I'm looking at her.

"Ever since the Ethnic Food Festival, I've wanted to try that recipe." I look at the clock. "Don't you have to pick up Olivia?"

"Actually, my mum is picking her up tonight so I don't have to be anywhere until bedtime."

"So you are free for two hours? Do you want to grab a drink?" She nods. "Let's go." I head to my car and don't look back. I know she will follow me to my apartment. I work my way through the last cars of rush hour and make it to my apartment in less than fifteen minutes. I unlock the door and leave it open because I know she will be here soon. I open a bottle of wine and pour two glasses. I don't know if we will even get to them so I take a quick sip. I look up and see her standing in my doorway.

"That was quite the look you gave me today in class. Whatever was on your mind?" She shuts the door and locks it behind her.

"I was thinking about our last night together and how you woke me up." I'm not shy with her. She smiles at me.

"It's hard to teach when you look at me like that." She comes over to me and takes my wineglass out of my hand, carefully placing it on the counter. "Take off your jacket." I unbutton my jacket slowly, never breaking eye contact with her. I have a feeling I'm still going to be the student even though class is over. My heart is hammering in my chest. "Now take off mine." She's wearing a suit jacket and I can't wait to feel her skin again. I get as close to her as I can, my lips inches from hers, and slide my hands between our bodies. I unlatch the button and slide my hands up to slip it off of her shoulders. I lean into her wanting to taste her lips, but she leans back preventing the kiss. I lick my lips in anticipation. "Take off your shirt." She looks down at my erect nipples and must know that I'm not wearing a bra. I don't hesitate. She reaches out and runs her thumb across my nipple. I gasp at how sensitive it is. She leans over and sucks it into her mouth. She slides her hands down and unbuttons my pants. "Go ahead and step out of them." She keeps me steady as I kick them across the floor. Her hands skim my body. "You're beautiful." She turns me around. I let my hair down because I know she likes to dig her fingers in it. "Get up on the counter." I hop up and she stands between my legs. I watch as she runs her fingers up my thighs and stops at my panty line. "These are coming off." I lift up my hips and she slips them off. She reaches over and takes a drink of wine. I watch her lick her lips and I just can't take it anymore. I pull her toward me and kiss her hard.

"No more teasing." I wrap my legs around her waist, trapping her against me. I quickly unbutton her blouse, ripping off the last button. I don't apologize. I need to feel her skin against mine. She's wearing a camisole and a bra. "Why are you wearing so much clothing?" I'm frustrated. "Can we go back into my room?"

"Not yet." She leans forward and licks my stomach, running her tongue down to my thighs. I lift my hips up when she gets closer to my pussy. Her warm tongue splits my folds and finds my clit immediately. I moan as she devours me. The counter isn't comfortable so I lean back on my elbows to better support myself. I watch her, my eyes half closed, as she spreads me open with her hands and buries her face in me. Thank God I don't have to be quiet. I couldn't if I tried. It's amazing to me how well she knows me, how to bring me to orgasm so quickly. I know we don't have a lot of time, but I hang on for a few seconds longer. Her mouth is incredible. When she slides a finger inside of me, I lie all the way back. It's the only way I can stop from orgasming right away.

"You're so wet, love," she says.

I push against her hand finding a nice rhythm. My moans are getting louder, and my hips are moving faster. I come loudly and wonderfully against her mouth and hand. My back is killing me, my legs are shaking, but I feel fantastic. I sit up because it hurts too much to stay horizontal.

"Well, this is one more reason to love a kitchen," I say.

Taryn leans up and kisses me, intensifying the moment. I've never been kissed so thoroughly before. Her tongue is warm, wet, and promising. I slide down off of the counter and she pulls me to her, holding me firmly. I break the kiss only because I want to get her back into my bedroom.

"We have about an hour," she says. I kiss her all the way down the hall, trying to take off her clothes as we head for the bed. I fumble around and she finally helps me so that the only thing left between my skin and hers is a pair of very sexy and very wet, white panties. We fall on the bed, and I waste no time touching and tasting her everywhere. Her body is responsive and she pushes into my touch wanting more. I run my tongue over her breasts. Her hands guide my head to her nipple. I greedily suck and lick her until she starts panting, and moaning. She is squeezing her other breast. As much as I want to sit up and watch her please herself, the need to taste her is too great. As my hand moves from her breast down to her stomach, she orgasms. I look at her in complete surprise. I've never been with a woman who orgasmed only from giving her breasts attention.

"Oh, my God, Taryn," I say. She's breathing hard as her body is trying to slow down. I keep my hand on her stomach until I feel her body settle, the quivers subsiding.

"Well, that's never happened before." Her voice is shaky and I'd smile if I wasn't so incredibly turned on right now. I lean up and kiss her slowly, deeply enjoying the feel of her full lips against mine. I slip my hand inside of her panties and start massaging her entire pussy. I am not gentle. She bucks up against my hand, her swollen lips wet and hungry for me. I slip inside of her and moan as her smooth walls grab me, pull me inside. I must be in heaven. Every time we're together, I fall a little bit more. I move inside of her, with her, because of her. Her second orgasm is even more delicious as I control it and drag it out.

CHAPTER TWENTY-ONE

I can't help but smile as I watch Taryn slide into my car. She's leaving her car for her mother so I spent last night cleaning mine out, vacuuming up crumbs, and anything else the hose could suck up that I no longer wanted in my car. I wiped down all surfaces, added an air freshener, and spot treated stains. It looks great.

"I'm excited." She reaches out and squeezes my hand before shutting her door.

My grin grows. "Me, too." I carefully merge into traffic and we're on our way to the lodge. I packed a cooler of snacks because as a chef, I can't help myself. Most people pack cookies and chips and soda for a road trip. I've packed cucumber sandwiches, turkey club pinwheels, and almond puff bars. I pay attention to what Taryn likes to taste.

"How was Olivia this morning when you left?" I'm almost afraid to know.

"She's so happy Grandma is in town that she barely waved good-bye." She exaggerates her frown. I kiss my forefinger and place it on her lips. She surprises me by holding my finger against her mouth and kissing me back.

"She'll miss you, but you'll be back tomorrow night. Plus, you can call her whenever, and she can call you." She keeps my hand in her lap and threads her slender fingers with mine. My heart catches, then races. My hand isn't at a very comfortable angle, but no way am I pulling it back. I'll take every crumb of affection she throws my way.

"True. So, what plans do you have for us today?" I lift my eyebrow at her. I feel a quick pulse of a squeeze as her fingers clench mine. "What else?" She doesn't know that I plan on keeping her in bed for the next thirty-six hours, but she seems to want more so I improvise.

"I packed us a light picnic for our bike ride today." Sure, the food is for the road trip, but I can pretend I made it for a private lunch.

"Ooh. What did you make us?" She's so cute.

"You'll just have to find out."

"I can't wait until I can cook for you. Just us. Not me teaching a class, but a date night." Interesting. Now we're dating. "After school is out, of course."

"I can't wait either." Her palate is as delicate as mine, and the two of us in the kitchen is going to be explosive. I shiver just thinking of the possibilities. I wonder if we'd ever get around to eating the food. Food is decadent. Feeding it to someone as sensitive as Taryn would lead to sex every time. We spend the two hour drive talking about education. She's fascinated about law school, and I prod her for information about her James Beard Finalist nod.

"Priorities change. I know I can cook. I learn new things every day. I was torn between a normal life with Olivia, and becoming a renowned chef. I made the decision to have a child, and it wasn't fair to her that others were raising her. I'll just spend the next twelve years perfecting cooking, and when she goes to college, I'll make a dramatic comeback." She looks peaceful, and I know she means it.

"Olivia is very well adjusted. For her upbringing, and all of the changes so far, she's doing a remarkable job of adapting."

"I think she's happy. She has friends at school, and gets good marks. Well, for a first grader."

"She just needs a kitten or two."

Taryn groans. "I know."

The lodge is remarkable. A bit more commercial than advertised, but still very serene. Taryn surprises me by wanting to go for a bike ride immediately instead of a quick make out session on the oversized canopy bed. I want to pout, but I remind myself that Taryn doesn't get the opportunity to do adult things very often. We head downstairs and rent two cruisers. I get one with a basket so that I can carry our picnic. It doesn't take me long to figure out that she is a cycling enthusiast. Her body was made for cycling. Tall, smooth, lean, and sinewy. I could look at her all day. Since we're at a snail's pace, we forgo the helmets. I promise her that I won't fall, and she promises me that she won't push me. I grew up on country roads. We used bicycle helmets to carry frogs, rocks, and anything we deemed absolutely necessary as part of our daily adventure. A helmet on my head feels foreign to me.

"I have to so that Olivia wears hers, too. She's still very awkward, and tends to forget she's riding a bike when she is looking around. We've had a trip to the emergency room already," Taryn says.

"I fall apart when Sophia sneezes and I have to take her to the vet. I can't even imagine how hard it is when a child is hurt."

"It's the worst thing ever. At least now she's old enough and can tell me when she is hurt or not feeling well. When she was a baby, I was a complete wreck whenever she cried. I didn't know if she was hungry, tired, teething, or if she caught some horrible virus. Of course my mind always went to the latter." I laugh. My mom is constantly telling me that, too. "Do you want children?" That question completely knocks me off guard, and I momentarily lose my balance. She laughs at me. "I guess that's a rather personal question."

"I would like to have a family someday. I don't know that I would want to physically birth a child, but I could adopt, or if my wife wanted to get pregnant, I would be fine with that." I sound more mature about the subject than I really am. Secretly, I'm scared to death, but all of my married friends tell me that when I find the right woman, the anxiety disappears.

"Being pregnant isn't for everybody." She doesn't elaborate so I assume she doesn't want to go through it again. This conversation is going down a path I'm not ready to think about just yet. This relationship is supposed to be casual, yet I'm picturing her pregnant again. I shake my head, trying to rid myself of that image.

"Are you getting hungry yet?" I ask. We've been riding for almost an hour. The trail we are on is paved and dotted with picnic tables every half mile or so. "We can pull over there and have a quick lunch." I point to a table in the shade. It's a warm spring day and I want to get out of the sun. I didn't pack sunscreen and I can feel the slight pinch of a burn tingling my shoulders and arms. I'm surprised that my legs feel strained.

Taryn nods and we pull off the trail. She grabs the picnic basket and peeks inside. "Smells delicious." She orders me to sit down and unpacks the basket, smelling all the food she puts in front of us. The almond bars bring a smile to her face. "Ah, dessert. I don't get to taste your desserts very often." I choke on my water. I can't tell if she's aware of the innuendo, but my body heats up. Her look is unreadable and just when I think she's innocent, she winks at me. I'm ready to take her behind the trees.

"You are such a tease." She laughs at me, knowing full well that I'm completely turned on and having a hard time relaxing. She fixes me a plate and I mask my surprise. I'm not used to thoughtfulness from my lovers. I find I'm holding my breath as she chews a pinwheel. I think I will always worry about what she thinks about anything I make. I'm eating the cucumber sandwich first. I've layered extremely thin slices of cucumbers with equally thin tomatoes, held together by a homemade three pepper hummus spread. It's tasty, but easy enough to make. The pinwheels were a bit harder. She closes her eyes for moment and lists off the ingredients. Surprisingly, she only gets about two thirds of them right.

"Your tongue must be off today," I say. She looks at me, her eyes narrowing. I can't help but smile.

"Well, then I will have to taste something I'm familiar with to get it spot on again."

"I think I can help you with that."

She leans over the table and cups my face. She looks into my eyes and slowly moves her lips closer to mine. My eyes close in anticipation. When her lips find mine, I sigh. It turns quickly into a moan as she dips her tongue inside my mouth, teasing me, tasting me. I want her closer. I grab her shirt and pull her to me, sucking her tongue into my mouth, not caring that we are in public and people can see us. Her hands drop down to my neck and slip inside my button down shirt, her fingertips pressing into me. She strokes my collarbone, her touch gentle, almost a whisper across my skin. I'm struck with an urge to cry at her tender, yet possessive control of me. This is what I want. This is what I've been waiting for. In the span of a single kiss, I have fallen into an unrecognizable place and I have no idea how to stop. I feel my own panic and pull away from her.

"I guess this isn't the place, huh?" she says. I nod and slowly sink down onto the bench. I can't feel my legs and my heart is throbbing in my chest. What just happened? I can feel tiny beads of sweat form up by my hairline and I quickly wipe them away. "Are you okay?" I nod and my laugh is shaky.

"Apparently I needed to get out of the sun for a bit," I say.

She hands me a cold water bottle. "Drink this, all of it. I don't want you to have heat stroke." I take the water and drink as much as I can. She wets a napkin and puts it on the back of my neck. The cold snaps me out of my almost meltdown and I'm able to relax again.

"Thanks." She watches me carefully and I try brushing it off. "I'm fine. Really." She lifts an eyebrow, but continues to monitor me. I'm hoping food will help so I pop a pinwheel in my mouth. "You failed on the ingredients test." She tastes another one and manages to get all of the components this time, except the dusting of paprika.

"I would have never thought of that. It's quite good." She eats another one and smiles as the final ingredient makes an appearance. "Got it." A smile blossoms on her face, her white teeth peeping out from beneath her full lips. I could drown in all of her.

"A clever trick I picked up during a condiment lesson several years ago."

"What has been your favorite class over your culinary career?" she asks.

"Well, I love the freedom that you give us in class so it's hard not to say yours."

"Okay, let me rephrase the question. What is your favorite thing to cook? Surely you have a favorite thing. I know I do."

"Here's the diner coming out in me, but I really do love to fry chicken. Yes, it's all about timing and ensuring your chicken is cooked all the way through, but it's also about the batter. The taste is a mixture of the crispy, spicy batter and the juiciness of the meat. There's just something so peaceful about it."

"Your chicken is really good, but your answer surprises me. I thought your soufflé was spot on and delicious. You looked confident the entire class."

I snort. "I was completely flying by the seat of my pants." She looks at me like I'm crazy. "Really. I added the flash mushrooms on top because the soufflé looked awful." She laughs, the lilt of her voice makes me smile even bigger. "Maybe I shouldn't be telling you all of my mistakes and screw ups since the final is coming up."

"Trust me, what happens here and outside of class, stays outside of class." I know she is serious and I nod at her. The final will be exciting. I do know that the scholarship contenders will have an extra cooking assignment. I brush the final away from my mind. I'm down to thirty hours with Taryn now and I don't want to waste them thinking about school. She reaches out for an almond bar and takes a bite. "I swear you're going to make me fat."

"My goal is to make you happy, not fat."

"I'm very happy with you," she says.

So what does that mean? Are we still casual? Have we turned the corner into something deeper? I want to ask more, but I'm afraid I'll come across as needy so I drop it. "I'm glad."

We finish off most of the food and pack it up, ready to continue our trek. I'm ready for aloe vera and a shower. She's ready for another ten mile ride. The things we do for love. Wait.

What? No. I'm not in love with her. I can't be in love with her. Have I even been in love before? I'm in that stage right before total panic sets in. My mouth feels dry, but sweat beads my forehead and upper lip. I can hear myself breathing so hard I sound winded.

"Are you okay?" Taryn is suddenly right in my line of vision. "You just turned white as a ghost. Maybe we should sit down again." She runs her hand up and down my back in a consoling way and walks me to the bench. "Here, drink this."

I gulp the water down and try hard not to hyperventilate in front of Taryn. This isn't supposed to happen. This is supposed to be fun only. In my mind, I'm in Italy this time next month, hitting on beautiful Italian women, and eating fantastic food. Images of me texting Taryn and holding my cell phone for a reply even though there is an eight hour difference flood my mind instead. No, this isn't good. I can't look at her right now. I'm sure it would show in my face.

"Put your head down," she says. Fine by me. I have an excuse to look away. Her soft touch is relaxing me and I'm able to slow down my breathing.

"Did I just sound like a husky?" She laughs, but I still hear an edge of concern in her voice.

"There was some heavy panting, but not the kind I find adorable. Maybe you've been in the heat too long?" She brushes the hair away from my face and I will myself to relax. A good five minutes passes before I am able to act as if I wasn't just shaken to my very core. "Want to head back?"

"No. I think I'll be fine. Besides, we're at about the halfway mark anyway. I'm sure I'll be able to make it without further embarrassing us both." I shake my head and am very near tearing up at my meltdown. Taryn puts her arm around my shoulder and pulls me closer to her. She smells like fresh laundry and honey.

I'm sure I smell like sweat and fear. The need for a shower pushes me up to a standing position. "I'm fine. The water helped. Don't let me ruin this day, okay?"

She nods and we clean up the picnic. A couple on a tandem bike ride by and Taryn stops them to score some sunscreen for me. She thinks it's heat stroke. I know it's heart stroke. When you read about people who fall in love or watch it happen in movies, it's all about smiles and tears of joy as two people cling to one another in sudden realization of this magnificent force. What the fuck happened to me? I feel heavy, physically and emotionally, and my tears are not that of happiness. Taryn looks alarmed and I feel scared. Granted, I haven't shared the news with her so that's not really fair to say. I told her this would be casual, and fun, and I can't change that this late in the game.

We have finals in a week and I need to keep it together until after the scholarship recipient is announced. If I don't win, then maybe we can talk about this relationship and the direction it's heading. Then maybe we'll have our happy tears. "I'm good now. Really." I jump on my bike and do a couple of circles around her until she seems satisfied that I won't fall or pass out. She takes the basket this time and we finish our ride without any further freak outs. Our conversation feels strained because I know she is still worried about me.

"I learned to ride a bike when I was three. I've always loved to ride. I even did a few bicycle tours in Scotland and Ireland during college."

I drove the three blocks to college every day even when the weather was nice. "That's why you are in such great shape."

She gives me a genuine smile for the first time in an hour. "Thank you." She's confident in the kitchen, the bedroom, but not overly confident with compliments.

I'm starting to feel normal again. My objective is to get her back to the lodge for much needed adult time. That's why we're here in the first place. By the time we check the bikes back in, I'm ready to run for the room. First to shower, second to seduce her the best way I know how. The concierge takes her time explaining where dinner will be and what time it's being served. I'm crushed that there is no room service. Since lunch was mainly finger foods, I'm hoping to talk Taryn into an early dinner so that our evening is free to explore one another. I calmly let us into the room and ask if she would mind if I showered first. She's insistent on it.

"Hopefully, it will make you feel better," she says.

I gather up a few essentials and head for the shower. I'm surprised, but grateful that Taryn doesn't pop in on me. Maybe we will shower together later tonight, or in the morning. I spend a few moments under the heavy stream of hot water coming to terms with my revelation today. I don't know whether to be angry with myself for falling in love, or happy about it, or just try to forget about it. Our future is completely up in the air and I'm clawing and scratching for answers. What now? Does she love me, too? Do I even tell her? Is this really love or just infatuation? What happens if I leave? What happens when I leave? I can't expect her to wait for me and I don't know that I would want my time in Italy stifled because of a relationship. That sounds selfish, but I've never been in love before and I'm only using my past experiences and behavior to guide me. I finally get out of the shower, deciding it would be a nice gesture to leave some hot water for Taryn, and get dressed. I still don't have the answers.

❖

Dinner is a buffet style gathering with all of the guests. Surprisingly, I find myself having a great time with our table companions even though the clock is ticking. Taryn is very charming and I don't want to take this away from her. Once they find out she is a renowned chef, they have tons of questions for her on how to cook certain foods. We aren't prepared when people ask about our relationship. I'm like a deer in headlights and after a few seconds of fumbling, she replies that we are cooking mates and came up here to unwind and have others cook for us instead. Everybody laughs and nobody questions us further about our relationship. I can't tell if I'm sad by her explanation of our relationship, or relieved.

We are served chicken fried chicken, rice with broccoli, a corn bake dish, homemade biscuits, corn on the cob, and mashed potatoes. Taryn and I are the thinnest ones at the table. I know she isn't going to eat a lot, but I dig in. The food is good, under-seasoned, but that's to be expected when cooking for a large audience. I reach for salt and pepper, wishing I could get my hands on some other spices. I've learned to not be a snob when eating other people's food though. I find out that peach cobbler with vanilla ice cream is the dessert tonight. Nobody can screw up peach cobbler.

"Is this too rustic of a meal to cook for a final?" I ask her. She looks at me in surprise. I know she isn't supposed to help me and I'm really not looking for help, just her advice. I give her a few moments to gather her thoughts before I try explaining myself.

"I can't imagine you would want to take your three years of experience at the academy to cook fried chicken. Yes, your chicken is amazing, but will it win you the scholarship? Picture yourself a judge and ask what would impress you on the panel?"

I guess that answers that question. Don't make fried chicken. After thinking about it, I nod. I smile at her. I now have a plan if she allows us to cook whatever we want.

"I take it you have something else in mind?" she says.

"Does it have to be from this semester?" I ask.

"No. The final for the scholarship will be using any skill you've learned during your education at the academy. I might make it easy for the rest of the students and tell them to make me something they've learned during my lessons."

"Do you seriously not know what our final will be? Not that I want to know but it is coming up."

"I have a meeting with the culinary board Tuesday and will present my ideas. We'll come up with a plan and I'm sure once it's finalized, the plan will be shared with the three of you. I will make it a stipulation that you cannot bring a recipe to class. It has to be from memory." That doesn't surprise me. I like it better that way. Most chefs do not have recipes hanging on the walls to help them unless it's Grandma's old recipe, or one that isn't used a lot. I already know that Scott will cook something from his parents' restaurant. He really should cook his wood fire brisket. The best I've tasted anywhere, but I'm not about to tell him that. I want to win this scholarship. Or do I? I find that losing isn't the worst thing that could happen to me. I would have to get a job somewhere besides Bud's Diner and I would see Taryn all the time. Two things that sound like pretty good consolation prizes. We would have to talk about whatever this relationship is and figure out how far we want to take it. She seems to still be in the casual stages of the relationship, but sometimes I catch her staring at me with such intensity that my knees threaten to buckle. Something squeezes inside of me and I have to take a deep breath just to move past that look.

"We can go back up to the room, if you want." Dinner is over and even though they are ready to serve dessert, I automatically stand before I answer her. "I guess that's a yes." She excuses us and we head upstairs.

I can't wait to touch her again. I've waited all day to feel her in my arms, dive into her warm and welcoming body. I steal tiny touches, gentle strokes all the way to the room. I want her explosive by the time we reach the door. I grab her by the elbow and twirl her back to me, her lips only inches from mine. I don't kiss her though. I look at her. Her pupils dilate and her breathing becomes heavier. I lick my lips in anticipation of her taste again. Her lips will be soft and sweet against mine, her skin slightly salty and tingly. I release her elbow and run my hand down the curve of her waist and over her hip before pulling her against me. I hear her exhaled breath right before my lips claim hers, aggressively and fully. She lifts her hands up to the back of my head and holds me in place and we duel for control of the kiss. I'm ready to drop to my knees and bury myself in her right there in the hallway, but we're suddenly interrupted by the ding of the elevator down the hall and break apart.

"Let's get back to the room," I say.

She nods and grabs my hand. We only have about twenty feet, but the door seems so far away. The couple who got off of the elevator go into their room so it's just us again in the hallway. She keeps a firm grip on my hand. It's as if she knows that if she lets go, I will fuck her right here in the open, up against the wall or somebody's door and that probably wouldn't be good for her reputation. As aggressive as she is, I think tonight she might not win. I have too much energy that has been building up all day and I'm done waiting. She unlocks the door and keeps walking straight to the bed. I'm one step behind her. I put my arms around her the second she reaches the bed and pull her hard against me. She moans and presses into me, her ass grinding against me. I reach down, my fingers finding her pussy and massage her through her dress, through her panties. I feel her legs give out and grab her waist to hold her up before I flip her to face me and push her onto the bed. I'm on her in an instant. She's trying to get my shirt off and I'm trying to get my hands on her bare thighs. Eventually, she submits and I'm able to slow down. Our kiss is deep and she arches into me when she thinks I'm pulling away.

"I want our clothes off," I say.

She relaxes against me again as I slide her panties down her legs. I spread her and lie between her legs, slowly pressing myself into her. She bends her knees up to gather more friction from my deliberately slow thrusts. She helps me unbutton my shirt and I'm very well aware of her hand resting on my heart while I shrug out of my clothes. She swallows hard and closes her eyes when my fingertips finally find her wet opening. Her pearly stickiness coats my fingers as I move two in and out of her. I watch her breath catch every time I push deep into her and feel her exhale on my cheek when I pull out. She's beautiful. As much as I enjoy listening to her soft and sensual moans, I enjoy kissing her more. I lean down and capture her lips in a fierce kiss. I can feel her desperation to come. She's just on the edge of orgasm. Encouraged, I move faster, deeper, harder. She breaks the kiss and cries out, bucking against my hand. I'm amazed at how fast and hard she climaxes. I place tiny kisses on the side of her neck until I feel her body settle. She shakes periodically, but I know it's not because she's cold.

"I love sex with you." She pushes the hair out of my face. "You know exactly how to touch me."

My response is a soft kiss on her bruised lips. I can't open my heart up to her yet, if ever. It's not fair to either one of us. The only thing I can do is show her how I feel without saying the words. I stand and carefully strip off our remaining clothes. I take my time touching her, knowing we have all night, and we won't be bothered until check out time tomorrow. She rests her hand on top of mine as I touch her everywhere. She's not guiding me, just staying with me, a deeper connection as I continue my seduction. I kiss my way down to the junction of her thighs and gently run my tongue up and down the soft, sensitive skin where her thighs meet her pussy. I'm slowly building her up again, only this time with more emotion. I don't know how to touch her without it now. Her fingers are wound in my hair, massaging me as I bring her to another orgasm. This one is different. I can just tell. She's holding me tighter, longer. I'm afraid to look at her so I crawl up and pull her into my arms. She doesn't fight me, but nestles deeper into the crook of my arm.

"Your heart is beating fast," she says. I nod. There's no need to say anything. Her fingers flutter over my body, soft touches across my stomach and breasts. I watch as she touches my nipple, pinching it into a hard pebble and easing the throbbing ache with her cool tongue. She's in no hurry this time and I let her take over. She does not disappoint. For probably the first time, I relax and give myself to her. I hang onto my orgasm until it crashes over me and even then I fight it. I want to feel this closeness, this sharing of bodies, and profound passion. I know that she has to feel something for me even if it's not love. Extreme fondness maybe, but nobody connects like we do without deeper emotions happening. Every time she's brought me to orgasm, she smiled at me after. She's not smiling this time. I don't question her, but I snuggle up to her and she holds me. The room smells like sex. I could use another shower, but there is something so decadent about smelling like your lover, that I'm able to easily fall asleep.

❖

I wince at the sunlight spilling into the room. Taryn is still fast asleep beside me, her hair piled up on the pillow. I'm not used to sleeping with a woman with long hair so it's going to take some getting used to. It's six in the morning. Check out isn't for another five hours. I slip from the bed and quietly take another shower and brush my teeth. Taryn is still asleep when I get back. I really don't want to wake her. She looks so peaceful and I know she doesn't get the opportunity to sleep in. I watch her sleep, falling in love with her even more with every breath I take. I'm so torn right now. I want to tell her, but I can't. We need to keep this casual until after the final or when I get back from Italy. She stirs a bit and snuggles closer to me. I think my wet hair wakes her up. She blinks at me and looks around. She smiles.

"Good morning." She stretches, the sheet exposing her breasts. She doesn't do a thing to cover up. I watch her and try not to get turned on, but fail miserably. She leans over and kisses me quickly. "I'll be right back." She slides off the bed and stumbles to the bathroom, not very gracefully.

I hear the shower and realize she won't be back for several minutes. I take the time to check messages and emails on my phone. Jessie doesn't even know where I am this weekend. I told her I was going to visit my mom, but she didn't call out my bullshit. She knows I can only take my mom for small periods of time. A weekend would probably be the death of me. I notice the time and try to plan out the rest of our time together. We can have breakfast in twenty minutes with everybody else, or we can stay in the room until check out and grab lunch somewhere on the way back home. Taryn wants to be home by five. Surprisingly, Olivia didn't call last night so Taryn had to call her to say good night. I kept quiet because I know she wants to keep the relationship private from Olivia. At least for now. I don't think Olivia will have a problem with us. She was around a ton of lesbians at the concert so she knows that sometimes women date. And plus she likes me. This might change if she ever finds out that her mom and I are dating. I know children don't like to share sometimes, especially a parent's attention. And since she only has Taryn, it might be difficult for her to make the transition.

"What would you like to do for breakfast?" Taryn asks. She's dressed in only a towel and is drying her long hair, completely oblivious to how sexy she is.

"Hmm. You don't really want me to answer that, do you?"

She crawls on the mattress toward me. "I believe we have time for whatever you want."

I grab the towel and yank her on top of me. We have plenty of alone time left before we have to leave.

Chapter Twenty-two

Can I please see my scholarship contenders?" Taryn asks. The three of us stop what we're doing and head over to her. I'm so excited, I have to stop from skipping. We're going to find out our assignment. "The final will be the same for everybody except you three." We all look at each other in surprise. "I talked to the members of the board and they want you to incorporate what you have learned this semester along with what you've learned the entire time you've been here and make a three course meal. You will be plating five plates. I'll be judging you by what you cook with the techniques I've taught you this semester and the rest of the judging will be on taste and previously taught methods. Dr. Wright, Ms. Dotson, Mr. Stewart, and J.D. will be the other judges. Are there any questions or concerns?"

"Is that fair since they haven't been with us this entire semester?" Scott asks. Typical Scott.

"Just be spot on with taste and technique and it really shouldn't matter who is judging. These instructors have known you since the beginning and they talk. They're well aware of your progresses and accomplishments," Taryn says. They all know what Scott did at Murphy's. I'm going into this with an edge. Scott purses his lips and wisely keeps quiet.

"Do we get to practice this week at all?" I ask. Since I know to avoid fried chicken, I think of other dishes that explode with taste and are technically challenging. I need to focus on a complete meal that the judges will appreciate.

"Definitely. For three days, the entire class will work on whatever they want and I'll be around to help. You can focus on what you want as long as they fall in the guidelines I've just outlined." I nod. This is good news. "And if you want my opinion on anything, I'm here for you."

I'm already thinking about my menu. Last year, I tried chicken mole using a chili powder instead of cutting up several types of chilies and slow cooking the sauce. The chicken was great, but the sauce really lacked that spicy, authentic punch of chilies and chocolate. I'm seriously considering making it again, but the right way. I will make a dessert soufflé, either lemon or vanilla for Taryn to show her that I do pay attention in class. I haven't decided on the third plate. I have the best champagne dressing recipe so I'm leaning toward a salad. It's crisp, refreshing and since the chicken mole and soufflé are filling, I need something light.

"Will you review our menus for us, if we want?" Mary asks. I know she's nervous, but she's really improved this semester.

"Definitely. I'm still your instructor through all of this. Don't be afraid to come to me for help." She looks at me and I smile. "If you have something in mind, lay it on me. I'll tell you what I think, but know that you are free to do whatever you want."

Mary pulls her aside to discuss her menu, so Scott and I head back to our stations. I grab a piece of paper and start my menu. The salad will be a poached pear with blue cheese chunks and cilantro. Adding cilantro to my champagne dressing will get the judges' palates ready for the Mexican entrée. I opt for white rice for the chicken mole and a vegetable medley of peppers, zucchini, squash, onions, and tomatoes. I'll end the meal with a Mexican vanilla soufflé. I'm not sure why I'm going with a Mexican theme, but all of the dishes complement one another well. When Taryn gets to me, I look up and have to stop myself from reaching out to her and pulling her close.

"Chef, how's it going?" she asks.

I show her my menu and I can't tell if she's impressed or not. It's a great opportunity to openly watch her without having to worry about getting caught. Her hair is down today and I remember wrapping my hands in it yesterday. I notice a slight mark on her neck and I'm tempted to tease her about it. I smile at the memory of making it.

"So why chicken with mole sauce?" she asks. I don't really have an answer so I think for a bit.

"When I tried this last year, I didn't use fresh ingredients and it fell flat for me. With five hours' cooking time, I know I can do it. What do you think?"

"Are you comfortable serving such a spicy dish to your judges?" she asks.

"This is a cooking class and mastering spices is part of it. They should know they will have to eat spicy food at some point. I know you don't mind it and I know J.D. likes spicy. Dr. Wright will focus more on my technique. I think if I slowly bring taste into the salad and end it with the mildness of the soufflé, my mole dish can have heat. I'll be careful so that it's not overpowering." She nods and recommends that I add lime to the salad dressing to help bring the flavors together. I smile at her. Great idea. "I think this is a good menu."

She moves on to Scott. Suddenly, I want to know what the others are cooking. Mary will almost certainly win the dessert category, but I plan on practicing my soufflé today. I'll work on my mole sauce tomorrow so that by Wednesday I can work on the salad dressing and relax until the final on Thursday. Everybody else will be done by Wednesday. Thursday, just the three of us will have the kitchen. I check the supply of Mexican vanilla and am happy there is some left. I head to the refrigerator for the rest of the ingredients. I have soufflés ready to pop into the oven in no time. My recipe makes four so Thursday I will double it and have eight just in case one or more crashes and implodes. I have thirty minutes to kill so I head over to Mary to check out her menu.

"What are you thinking?" I ask. She shows me her menu. Lamb chops with ginger potatoes and her famous strawberry shortcake.

"I don't know what I should do for an appetizer. You have any suggestions?"

"Well, the lamb is rich so something with bread. Maybe something with crushed olives, oil, and feta or a milder cheese. You don't want too many flavors at once. Keep it simple and focus on the taste. Be sure to make me a plate on Thursday, too." She smiles at me and asks me about my menu. When I tell her chicken mole, she looks at me like I'm crazy.

"You can cook anything and you choose that? I mean, not that it's bad, it's just hard and that's kind of your Kryptonite." Mary was in my class last year when I tried it and obviously remembers my feeble attempts.

"I feel like it's unsettled between us."

"I want you to win. Maybe you should cook a nice filet. You did well at Murphy's," she says. I shrug. Grilling a piece of meat and watching a clock isn't hard. I want something that will push me. Either way, I win. If I'm chosen as the winner of the scholarship, I win. If I come in second, I still win. I win Taryn and our time starts the minute class stops. Maybe I'm purposely trying to sabotage myself so that I can spend more time with her. No, I'm too competitive to just give in, even for love. There's that word again. Maybe it's just infatuation because we both cook and we have a lot in common. "Other than the difficulty level, your menu sounds delicious. Make sure you save me a plate as well."

I wish her luck and head back to my station to clean up my mess. I still have twenty minutes until the soufflés are done. Not enough time to start something else, so I grab some chilies from the refrigerator and start dicing them up for tomorrow. Maybe cutting them a day early will help subdue the sting. I put gloves on before I start cutting them. I have a problem of rubbing my eyes a lot. Pepper in your eyes is horrible, even the mild ones.

Staying busy will keep me from checking on the soufflés every two minutes. They look good from the outside, but I know not to bump the oven at all. One tiny tremor and they could fall. I dice the peppers and still have time to kill. For whatever reason, Scott keeps walking by my oven and I start getting nervous. I end up guarding it again like I did last time we baked them. I'm sorely tempted to goad him, knock him off of his game a bit, but I want to win this fair and square. I want to show everybody that I'm better than he is, as a student, a chef, and a competitor.

"So you don't think chicken mole is a good idea? You kind of have a thing against chicken, don't you?" She laughs. I called Taryn even though I know her mother is there. It's nine thirty and I know Olivia is asleep.

"Silly girl. I think it's a good idea and I know you'll cook it well," she says.

"Any words of advice? Suggestions?"

"Don't use anything from a jar."

"Not even the Mexican vanilla?" I ask.

"Well, that's okay. I mean for the mole."

"I'm memorizing the recipe as we speak." Not really, but I want her to think so.

"There are about twenty to twenty-five ingredients in mole. You can't forget a single one."

My confidence is waning. "Trust me. I don't want to embarrass you or myself. I will have it down by Thursday. Mary's meal sounds good." I'm trying to change the subject. Everybody seems to be against this dish.

"It does, and you know I can't talk about it," she says. So there is a chef-chef confidentiality agreement that I know nothing about.

"I'm just telling you that we talked and shared menus."

"I know. I'm very much aware of you in class."

I perk up. I like this conversation better. Now, I'm nervous. Did I do anything embarrassing? "Why?"

"Why? What do you mean why?"

"Why are you aware of me?"

"Because you are a fantastic chef and I like watching you work," she says.

"Boo."

She laughs. "Really? Boo?"

"That was the teacher answer. I wanted the…" I pause before saying the word girlfriend. "…close friend answer." I draw out the word 'friend' to let her know I see us as more than that.

"I watch you because you are sexy and very confident in the kitchen. A woman who goes after what she wants and isn't afraid to try new things is very sexy."

"I agree. That's why I like watching you, too. When are we going to cook together?"

"Let's get through the final first. Maybe Friday night if you are up for it."

"That works great for me. Bud gave me Friday and the whole weekend off."

"Maybe I should just cook for you and you can be my guest," she says.

"Or maybe I can help you cook a meal for Olivia and your mother whose name I don't even know yet."

She laughs. "Evelyn. And she's going to love you."

I'm surprised that Taryn will have me around both her mother and her daughter. Now, I'm interested in how she will introduce us. Will I be a friend, a student, or a girlfriend? "From everything I know about her already, I'm sure we'll get along just fine." I already have a lot of respect for a mother who stands by her daughter through every decision. "What are we going to cook?" Taryn has a good sized kitchen and it will be nice to see how she cooks outside of the classroom.

"We need to make it Olivia friendly, or cook her something else," she says.

"Let's cook her something special. I want to cook adult food for us. Maybe we can cook something from South Africa?"

She laughs. "I don't think that's a good idea. Let's wait to do that after my mum leaves. She's here to eat American style food or food she can't get back home and I don't want to disappoint her. But don't worry about that menu. Just keep your final in mind and stay focused on mole."

"You know what's weird? I'm really not nervous. I love that we will have the kitchen to ourselves to cook on Thursday. I'll just go in thinking I have to cook dinner like it's my job."

"You have no reason to be nervous. Your cooking is superb and I have complete faith in you," she says.

"Do you know how it's going to be graded? Like by course or just overall?"

"This isn't Top Chef. We'll do it by complete meal. We won't know who will win the scholarship until Friday. They need to analyze all of your work throughout the three year program and then discuss the meal in detail including overall taste, appearance, technique, and anything else they can come up with. I'm excited to be a part of it even though I don't have the history on the three of you that the other judges do."

"Did you read our records when we started the semester?"

"Sure. I studied everybody's file, but focused on yours, Scott's, and Mary's."

I'm intrigued. "Anything you can share with me?"

She laughs. "Absolutely not. It was mostly good stuff."

"Mostly good? Mostly? That's awful. Now I'm going to be worried." She knows I'm joking. My record is perfect.

CHAPTER TWENTY-THREE

I was twenty-three years old and in Las Vegas when I first tasted champagne salad dressing. We were blowing off steam after a very difficult first year in law school so several of us decided to go to the city of sin for a long weekend. While my gay friends were hitting the strip clubs, and my straight friends were gambling, I was eating. I had lunch at a restaurant inside the Bellagio casino and ordered a salad that would forever change my life. I wanted to find out the ingredients, but was unable to get into the kitchen because I was just a customer. I wasn't a chef and I couldn't name drop because I didn't know anybody yet. Instead, I Googled all the different champagne salad dressing recipes and pulled together all of the possible ingredients and took notes on my phone. I asked the waiter for another salad with the dressing on the side and began my dissection.

When I got home, it took several tries before I was able to recreate it. Now, I have it down to a science. The right amount of cilantro and lime will take time so while the rest of the class is working on their final, I'm trying to tweak my perfect salad dressing. The first batch is horrific and I can't get the taste out of my mouth fast enough. If cilantro isn't presented in the right amount, it will leave a perfume taste. Apparently, I have too much in the dressing. I cut the amount of cilantro by half, add the lime juice and mix it again. It's better, but still strong. I don't want it to overpower the sweet crispness of the champagne, so I cut it back again. After cutting it again, I finally get the right mixture. I pull the ingredients together for my salad and poach the pears, toast the walnuts, and pour the dressing over it. It's too warm still and wilts the lettuce. Mental note, let the dressing cool first.

"Please make sure you give me a list of the ingredients you need, and I will make sure you have everything tomorrow," Taryn says.

My chicken mole recipe is quite lengthy and I know that we have several items here already. I'm sure Taryn will lock up the items we need so that others within the institution don't accidentally use them. Several people in the class have come up to wish me luck. Scott might be a favorite with some of the instructors, but he doesn't have the respect of his colleagues. Mary comes over with her list and asks me to review it. I love that she has such faith in me. I show her my menu and she shakes her head.

"God, Ki. You are one brave girl."

"I'm just glad we get the entire class to make the final. I'm sure Scott will be done in less than an hour. I bet he stays for all of it," I say.

"I hope that Taryn doesn't let him stay. It's her decision. I'm sure if he's a distraction, she will ask him to leave."

I nod. "He won't bother me though."

"Chef," Mary says. I think she's talking to me, but she's calling Taryn over to us.

"Yes, chefs?" Taryn asks.

"Are we allowed to stay for the whole class even if we get done before the time is up?"

"I hadn't thought about that yet. I guess as long as you aren't disruptive to the other students, it shouldn't be a problem." She seems surprised that students would want to support one another. Apparently, that isn't common in this industry. We hand her our lists and she starts gathering the ingredients until some students start plating for her. It's hard in this industry to not pass at this level. I know the students well enough to know that they all will do fine. I'm pretty much done so I clean up my station and decide to leave early. I wait until Taryn is done tasting and head over to her.

"Chef, I'm done prepping for the final. Is there anything you need from me before I leave for the day?" My back is to the class and I wink at her. She clears her throat to cover up her smile.

"No, you're good. Get some rest tonight. You have a very important day tomorrow."

"I'll see you tomorrow." I grab my bag and head out. I can feel her watching me and it takes all of my energy not to turn around.

❖

The knock on my door doesn't surprise me. I kind of expect it. I have two glasses of wine poured and ready.

"Are you expecting someone?" Taryn asks as she enters the living room.

"You. I hope you like Pinot."

"How did you know I would stop by?"

I close the door behind her and lock it. When she turns to face me, I greet her with a kiss. It starts out sweet, but escalates quickly and I have to pull away from her. I don't want her to think that I only want sex.

"Because you're sweet like that." I take her hand and we sit on the couch.

"I just wanted to see how you're doing."

I hand her the glass of wine. "I feel pretty confident about tomorrow." I'm still very calm. This is what I've been training to do for the last three years professionally and several years before that on my own. Taryn starts talking about her education and what her final was like. I think she's nervous for me. Not because she thinks I'll do badly, but because she thinks I'll do well. She plays with my fingers and I smile as she studies my hands.

"You have such soft, delicate hands," she says. I like how gentle she is as she runs her fingertips over my fingers. "And these hands create such magic." She's completely relaxed and I feel my heart flutter inside and race around my chest as I look at her. This is what I want. Us.

"You inspire me. I'm a good chef, but you make me want to be the best I can be."

"Your hands aren't just magical in the kitchen."

"Again, you inspire me."

She blushes. "Whatever happens tomorrow and Friday, just know that I've really enjoyed spending time with you. I know as an instructor, what I did was inexcusable—"

I cut her off. "It was my suggestion and it's not as if we're children. We're adults. I'm completely capable of making my own decisions. What we have here is not a bad thing at all and you shouldn't feel bad about us. I've enjoyed every minute of it."

"It's just totally unprofessional and I do feel guilty about it." I cup her face in my hands and shake my head.

"Don't. Don't do this to yourself or us. This has been incredible. Where else would we have met? A restaurant? Same situation. No dating at work. Maybe this was our destiny. Please don't feel bad about this. I need this. I need you." I lean over and kiss her gently. I put as much emotion into that kiss as I possibly can without crying or confessing my love for her. She is hesitant, but she is still here, still in my arms so I know she still believes in us. When I pull away and look into her eyes, she gives me a smile that doesn't quite reach her eyes. I kiss her again and again until I feel her smile against my lips and I know her mood has improved.

"See? You always know what to say or do to make me forget about my worries." She strokes my cheek.

We spend the rest of our time talking about simple stuff like what her mother and Olivia are doing the rest of the week and Sophia's life story. Sophia has a habit of curling up in Taryn's lap whenever she comes over. She's not even this lovable with Jessie. I know we're keeping the conversation light for Taryn's sake. I know she doesn't want to talk about our relationship until we find out what happens in two days. When she leaves, it takes five minutes before I actually let her walk out my door. At least she's smiling this time.

CHAPTER TWENTY-FOUR

The room is brimming with energy. The judges are getting set up and the three of us are getting ready to start.

"Students, you have five hours to prepare a three course meal for the five of us. You will be judged on the preparation, the taste, and presentation of your meal. You will not be allowed to use any notes or use your phones. Show us what you've learned over the past three years and impress us. You may begin," Taryn says.

I have to fight the urge to run to my station. I immediately gather up the twenty-two ingredients for the mole because it will require the most time and attention. It will take hours for the sauce to thicken and cook for the best flavor. When I made it the other night, it was delicious. I just need to do the exact same thing, no pressure. Taryn bought the best chicken possible and I smile when I pull it from the refrigerator. I see that Scott is making something with lobster. He should make his lobster bisque, but he's not touching them yet so apparently they are his main course. I think that's a mistake. Mary is in the zone. I'm so proud of her. She really stepped it up the last month. It's too bad she's not my toughest competition.

I look up after about an hour and a half and notice that both Mary and Scott have delivered their first plates and are working on entrées. I don't want to wait several hours between my plates. I want it to be restaurant style where I serve the salad, entrée, and dessert all within an hour's time. Taryn looks worried so I shoot her a quick smile. I know what I'm doing. I'm going to use all of my time wisely.

The champagne dressing is spot on and I let it cool down before I pour it. I'm trying not to let the stress of the competition get to me. The chicken mole still has to braise for another thirty minutes so I start cooking sticky white rice. I will plate the salad in twenty minutes, then twenty minutes after that, plate the chicken mole, white rice, and crisp vegetable medley. Thirty minutes after that, I'll serve dessert. Scott is serving his main course which looks like lobster pot pie. I've never tasted it, but I know it can be tricky like most seafood. The judges inspect the dish, smell it, gently break open the top and eat it. Even though I don't want to care, I can't stop watching them. Their reactions are hidden so I have no idea. I start on the soufflés and get them ready until I have to beat the egg whites. I've found that the fresher the soufflé, the fluffier the soufflé.

"Here's a plate for you." Mary slides a plate of lamb and ginger potatoes onto my station. I look it over, smell it, and catch myself doing exactly what the judges are doing. We aren't really supposed to talk so I dig into it instead of giving her my opinion. I don't love lamb, but it's perfectly cooked according to the institution's guidelines. The ginger potatoes have a slight sweetness that is nice and unexpected. She did a great job. I give her a thumbs up and get back to my meal.

It's time to plate the salad. I take my time and ensure that each dish is beautiful. The pears are perfectly poached and I have just enough blue cheese on the salad. I taste the dressing before I put it on the salad just in case it settled wrong. It's fantastic. I catch myself from doing a little happy dance. I'm about ready to blow their minds and their palates. I slide a plate over to Mary and take a tray to the judges. I explain my salad and dressing to them.

"Ki, why the long wait for a salad?" Dr. Wright can be a true asshole sometimes.

"I want to serve the meal as if you're in a restaurant. The salad first, then the entrée in twenty minutes, then dessert. My entrée takes longer to make than the others. I plan on using most of the time allotted for the final. I apologize for the wait." I nod and leave before they ask any more questions.

I need to get back to my mole and get my soufflés into the oven. Mary rubs circles on her stomach when I return to my station. She likes the salad. I give her a wink. I'm trying to gauge Taryn's reaction, but she is stoic like the rest of the judges.

I move on, getting back into my zone. The sticky rice is almost done. I mix my medley, waiting for a bit so that the marinade doesn't weigh down the vegetables. I want them to be crisp and clean. This entire dish won't look like I've spent hours on it, but if I nail the sauce, the judges will know and hopefully appreciate my efforts in creating such a complex taste.

Scott is presenting his dessert of plum pudding. It looks good, but his entire meal seemed heavy. Lots of creams and thick breads. He should have gone with the Irish theme since he didn't make his brisket.

I quickly taste the mole and decide the flavor is there. I'm ready for the final step. I add the mole to the roasted chicken and place it into the oven for an additional ten minutes to marry the flavors.

Mary delivers her strawberry shortcake to the judges. They're all smiling. I can't help but smile, too, because I know it tastes better than it looks, and it looks fantastic. She returns to her station and slides me over a plate. I want to taste it, but I need to plate my entrée.

I pull the pan from the oven and let it rest before I start preparing the plates. I taste it and almost weep with delight and relief. It's even better than a few days ago. I fix six plates, clean all marks off of the plates and deliver five of them to the judges. I explain my meal, why I chose chicken mole, and tell them to enjoy. I need to finish my soufflés and get them on the table in thirty minutes. Scott is still in the room and he snorts when he sees my entrée. Taryn points to the door. He grabs his bag and leaves, shaking his head. I can hear him laugh outside of the classroom, but I don't allow him to derail me. I know it's good. I know they will like it, too.

I say a little prayer when I fill the soufflé dishes, adding collars so that when they cook, they will be approximately two inches higher than the rim of the dish. I actually haven't tried this before so I'm glad I decided to make eight desserts altogether in case something goes wrong. I quietly add them to the heated oven and set the timer. Now, I just have to wait.

I spend my time cleaning up my station, stealing glances at the judges. They're taking bites and writing in their notebooks. I catch Taryn's eye, but she doesn't give me any hint on the entrée either. I keep the light on in the oven and check the soufflés every three minutes. I'm getting nervous because they are getting tall and I hope the collars stay in place. When the timer dings, everybody is watching me. They're either really nervous for me, or really excited for soufflés. I carefully take out the soufflés and place them on the station. I have six really pretty ones and two that self-destructed. I quickly dust the whole ones with powdered sugar and cautiously remove their collars. They're beautiful. I'm shaking and I have to take a moment to settle down. Mary comes over to help deliver them to the judges.

"These look gorgeous. Take a deep breath and let's go get your scholarship," she says. I release a pent up nervous laugh and carefully place the desserts on trays. We take baby steps to get them across the room. The judges are all smiling.

"Vanilla bean soufflé. I chose Mexican vanilla to stay true to the theme. The soufflés are light and should complete the meal nicely. Enjoy." I head back to my station to finish cleaning up. Mary follows me and I give her the sixth soufflé to try. She moans after the first bite. I almost cry with relief.

"This is better than my strawberry shortcake," she says.

"Nothing is better than your strawberry shortcake."

"You need to taste this." She hands me a spoon. I'm almost too nervous, but I dig in. My spoon bounces in the fluffy dessert. Perfect texture. I take a bite and smile. I nailed this. I nailed the entire meal. I finish cleaning up my station. Mary and I head over to retrieve our bags. Taryn finally looks at me and I nod at her. I want her to give me a sign or something to let me know how I did. I know she was nervous because I didn't serve until the others were already serving their desserts. I'm going to be right by my phone all night, waiting for her call. I take a deep breath and try to right myself. As I'm about to walk out of the class, the last class I will ever take at Kirkwood Academy, she winks at me.

Chapter Twenty-five

I skip to answer my door because I have so much energy from the final and am on such a high. Taryn's standing in my doorway with a bottle of champagne and a huge smile on her face.

"I can't even tell you how happy and proud I am." She kisses me fiercely.

"So you liked it, huh?"

She gives me the biggest, longest hug. "Fantastic. Absolutely delicious. The judges were blown away. Not too many students have tried chicken mole, let alone perfected it."

"Any issues with anything I cooked?"

"Nothing. Spot on tonight, spot on. Here, I bought this to celebrate. Oh wait, do you have other plans tonight?" She hands me the bottle. I'm not going to tell her that I shooed Jessie away claiming a really bad headache knowing full well Taryn was going to either come by or call me.

"No, no. Let's open it and you can tell me all about it. It's still very fuzzy to me." I don't remember a lot of the competition.

"Well, everybody was nervous because you weren't serving anything for hours. I had to tell them what you were making because they were a bit antsy. Once the food came out, they understood the delay. The salad was light and full of flavor. The dressing was a complete hit. I was afraid J.D. was going to lick his plate. When the chicken mole was served, we couldn't wait to dig in. It was perfectly balanced. The bittersweet chocolate subtly counteracted the spicy peppers and the rice helped lower the heat. The vegetables were light, crispy, and had an excellent marinade. You did great. Really a perfect meal."

I can't stop smiling. "How did everybody else do?" I hope she can share some information with me.

"Everybody else did a good job, too. Delicious flavors, but there were some errors that I can't discuss. I have to say, your soufflé was amazing. Most of the time, added flavors really weigh the soufflé down, but not yours."

I'm pretty sure I can sit here and listen to Taryn praise me all night. "I cooked eight soufflés and two committed suicide halfway through cooking them. I'm glad I thought ahead to double the ingredients and make as many as I could."

"I thought it was sweet that you and Mary shared your meals. Very thoughtful." She reaches out for my hand, anxious to touch me. She might actually be more excited than I am about the final.

"I'm actually ready for a cheeseburger and fries. I want something simple and easy and greasy that I don't have to make."

"Would you like to go to Bud's? I'm sure they are anxious to know how you did," she says.

"How late can you be out? What are your plans?"

"Olivia and my mum are at a movie right now. They won't be home until about eight. I'm sure after that there will be ice cream and games at home. I won't be missed for a while."

I scoot closer to her and kiss her softly. "I don't want to waste any time with you."

She looks at me for a moment, her eyes serious and her emotions guarded. "Tomorrow we can hang out for as long as you like. They're going to the zoo in the morning and I've told them that we are fixing them dinner so we will have most of the day and the night together if you would like that."

"Of course I would. Okay, then let's share a toast and grab some greasy food."

"I will probably only have a soda, or an iced tea, because I ate three dinners only an hour ago," she says.

"We can stay here and I can just make something real quick."

She looks at me. "You've been cooking all day. If you want a greasy cheeseburger, you will get a greasy cheeseburger."

I retrieve two champagne glasses from the kitchen while Taryn opens up the bottle. The cork pops off, scaring us. Sophia jumps about five feet and runs down the hallway, presumably to hide under the bed.

"Here's to my favorite student and her kick ass final," Taryn says. We clink glasses and she gives me a quick kiss. "Let's go satisfy your hunger."

❖

Bud's not working tonight, but the night crew is anxious to hear how the final went.

"Well, I won't find out about the scholarship until tomorrow, but I cooked my heart out." Val, Jennifer, and Peter, the night cook, are at the counter listening to my story. We share a round of high fives and I dig into my double cheeseburger and fries. Taryn looks at me and shakes her head.

"One day you won't be able to eat like this and keep your girlish figure," she says.

"So you'll only love me if I'm thin?" I ask. I stop mid bite as the words I just said sink in. Fuck. How am I going to get out of this one? She's as still as I am. "I mean, I have to be thin forever?" Fuck. This can't get any worse. "You know what I mean." I eat a couple of fries and refuse to make eye contact. We are thankfully saved by Val who swoops in to check on us. Thank you, Val.

"So what happens now? Are you going to stay here at the diner if you don't get the scholarship?" Not that her question helps me, but it at least gets us out of that very awkward moment.

"I will probably send my résumé out to some of the restaurants down in The District. I might even send it to Murphy's, the steakhouse we cooked in the other week." The District is the popular hot spot for dining, dancing, and drinking. There are about half a dozen five star restaurants and I'd be lucky to work in any of them.

"But if you get the scholarship, when do you leave?" she asks. I give her a look until it finally sinks in that she is having this conversation in front of the quasi-girlfriend I might be leaving for ten months. She blushes and stands back from the counter. "Oh, I'm being flagged down by a customer." She's gone in two seconds flat. All I wanted tonight was to eat a greasy cheeseburger and spend time with Taryn. Now we've got this heaviness between us that is squeezing my heart. I don't know what to do or say. I can only sit here and eat this food that is settling into my stomach like a stick of dynamite. Thankfully, she slips into teacher mode and starts talking again.

"I have a conference call in the morning with the judges and we're going to finalize the pick. Dr. Wright is going to either call or send an email to the scholarship recipient. He will ensure that all the proper paperwork is filled out and the forms will be sent to San Rocco School in Venice. You do have a very good shot." At least she glazed over the 'L' word and is pretending it didn't happen. It sounds too real with her telling me all of this. Food is no longer appealing and I put down my cheeseburger. "Are you done?" she asks.

"I guess I tasted too much food during the final. Can we get out of here?" I throw some money on the counter and we head out. We're fairly quiet on the ride back to my apartment. At least she gets out of the car and follows me inside instead of throwing the car into gear and screeching the tires to make a quick getaway.

"Want another glass of champagne or something else?"

"Sure. Let's continue the celebration," she says.

Pouring new glasses keeps me busy until I can settle down from the events of the last hour. We clink glasses again and I'm finally able to look at her for more than five seconds.

"So what happens for you this summer? How many classes do you have?" The academy is year round, so Taryn won't get as much of a summer break as she originally thought.

"I have two classes again. Dietary Management in the morning, and Pastries in the afternoon. Pastries doesn't run late so I will be done by three every day. Olivia will be happy because then we can go to the pool since I will get home early enough."

"Where will she be when school is out?" I ask.

"She'll be at Adventure Club at her school until I can pick her up. She's scheduled until six, but I will get her early most days."

"I want to go swimming with you. It would be nice to see you in a bikini." I scoot closer to her and give her a soft kiss. She laughs.

"I haven't worn a bikini since Olivia was born," she says.

"Are you kidding me? Why not? Look at you. You are gorgeous." She blushes. She really isn't good at receiving compliments. I take her glass and put it on the coffee table in front of the couch and straddle her lap. "Guess what?"

"What?" She is staring at my mouth and licks her lips in anticipation of our inevitable kiss.

"You're no longer my teacher," I say. She smiles at me.

"You're right." I stroke her cheek and run my fingers across her plump bottom lip.

"I love how full your lips are. Do you know that I probably spent more time in class focusing on your mouth than any other part of your body?" I exhale sharply as she captures my hand and presses a kiss to my fingertips.

"You were my biggest distraction and yes, I knew you were watching me."

"Everything about your mouth is incredible. Your lips are so red, so sensitive, and your palate is remarkable."

"Says the chef. Nobody else would say that to me," she says.

"Nobody else better say that to you," I say. She giggles. I lean in and give her a swift kiss. I really don't want this night to turn into another night of sex, but I have a hard time not touching her when she's this close, this available. "You probably need to get home, don't you?" She sighs against me.

"Probably. Mum is leaving soon and I need to spend more time with her. I don't know when I will see her again. Maybe Christmas."

I slide off of her lap and face her. "When do you want me tomorrow?" She reaches out and plays with a strand of my hair. I'm going to miss this closeness, her touch, her everything if I go to Italy.

"Whenever you're up and about. I want you to do a little bit more celebrating tonight. You deserve it. Call Jessie and your other friends and have fun," she says. Funny that I think this is celebrating. Just us. I walk her over to the door and kiss her one more time before I let her go.

"I'll text you in the morning," I say. She lingers in my doorway, kissing me softly, slowly. I'm two seconds from pulling her back inside.

"Have fun tonight. Tell your friends I say hello." She walks down the hallway and gives me a quick wave before she disappears.

CHAPTER TWENTY-SIX

M y cell phone rings and I ignore it. I squint and see that it's eight thirty. Jessie took me out last night and we didn't get back until two this morning. I swear I just went to bed. When the home phone rings, I sit up. Very few people have my home phone number so I know it's either an emergency, or a telemarketer who is about to hate his or her job.

"Hello?" My voice sounds raspy and foreign so I clear it, which only makes me sound like an eighty-year-old man.

"I'm trying to reach Katherine Blake." I sort of know the voice, but my head is too foggy to process.

"Speaking," I say. Or mumble. I'm not quite sure.

"Ki? This is Dr. Wright from Kirkwood. Is this a bad time?" My heart starts beating fast and I realize this is the call I've been waiting for. I clear my throat and reach for the water that is magically beside my bed. Thanks, Jessie.

"One moment." I mute the phone, take a drink, and clear my throat. "Sorry about that. I'm back."

"Sounds like you might have celebrated last night."

I sort of chuckle. Get to the point, man. He pauses, so apparently I'm to respond. "Yes. My best friend took me out last night and I didn't have to work this morning."

"Well, I'm calling to congratulate you on being the winner of the Excellence in Culinary Arts Scholarship." He pauses again.

At least I'm smiling now and ignoring my pounding headache. "That's fantastic news, Dr. Wright. Thank you for calling and telling me." He's quiet, but I'm not kissing his ass.

"It was a very good meal you prepared and we all appreciated the time, effort, and skills used to create it. Scott was a close second." Now why did he have to add that during my glorious moment? Why couldn't he just leave Scott out of this entirely?

"It's nice to be recognized by my instructors. What has to happen now?" I ask.

"Well, come in early next week and we'll sign the forms and get them to San Rocco." And we are quiet again.

"Okay, I'll do that. Thank you again." Finally, he gets the hint and hangs up. I'm too pumped right now to go back to sleep, but I still have a serious hangover so I crawl back under the covers. I can text people instead. I text Jessie, Lynn, Bud and a few others. I don't want to text Taryn. She knows by now. I need to call her. And my mom. I need to call her now.

"Hi, Mom." My mom is already at work and has probably had four cups of coffee by now.

"What's wrong? You sound horrible. Are you okay?"

"Yes, I'm good. I just wanted to let you know that I won the scholarship and I'm going to Italy early next month." I realize I probably should have told her in person. My mom is going to have a hard time with me gone for ten months.

"Oh, honey, that's great news." She sounds genuinely happy. "I'm so proud of you."

"Thanks. I won't know the details until next week, but I wanted to let you know first." She doesn't need to know I texted my friends and my boss before I called her. We talk for a bit longer and I tell her I have to go. We make plans to have lunch on Sunday. My phone blows up with my friends' congratulatory wishes. I even have a text from Bud. I revel in their kind words before I get serious and call Taryn. She answers almost immediately.

"Good morning," I say.

I can hear her smile. "Good morning, Ki." I will never get tired of her saying my name.

"I'm sure you know why I'm calling."

"You mean it's not just to say hello and make plans for today?" She's teasing.

"Well, that, too, but Dr. Wright called and told me I won the scholarship. Of course he made a point to mention Scott was a close second." That sets her off.

"What an asshole. He wasn't close at all. He came in a distant second for the scholarship, but Mary beat him at the final meal. I can't believe he said that to you. I will not let him get me, or you down. You were fantastic and totally deserve it. Congratulations."

"Thanks. One more thing to celebrate today. What time do you want me?"

"How about noon? I have to finish up a few things here at the academy. I can pick you up and we can plan the meal and go shopping." She congratulates me over and over until I finally say good-bye. I lie back down and snuggle under the covers, I'm happy, but my head is starting to pound. Thankfully, I still have three hours to sleep before I have to get up and get ready.

❖

"My mum loves lasagna. Do you want to make the noodles or buy them…" Taryn stops when she sees the disgusted look on my face. "Okay, we'll make them. I just thought maybe you wanted more time with me." I playfully pinch her side and she laughs. "With both of us cooking, we will knock this out in no time." We pick out ingredients for a quick salad with an Italian blend dressing. As much as I would like to bake garlic bread from scratch, I do want some time alone with Taryn so I opt for store bought. I grab a fresh mozzarella ball and tomatoes to slice up and serve before dinner. Taryn approves. We're out of there and back to her place within the hour. I'm having a hard time keeping my hands off of her as we climb the stairs to her apartment.

"Call your mom and find out when they will be home. Maybe we have a few minutes alone."

We put away the groceries and Taryn calls her mom for an update. Even though the call is only about three minutes, it feels more like fifteen. Always impatient and desperate for her, I pull her closer and start unbuttoning her shirt.

"So you won't be home for about an hour or so?" she asks. That should be enough time for me to show her how I feel without speaking. I pull her shirt from her slacks. She lifts her arms up out of the way so that I can unbutton her pants. She smiles at me as I help her out of them. "No, I don't need to talk to Olivia. I'll see her in an hour when you get home." Her mother simply isn't getting the hint. I run my hands down her sides, over her hips and pull her against me. She moans slightly at the contact and I go still when I hear her mother ask if she's okay. "Yes, I just ran into the counter. I'm fine." I run my fingers over the silkiness of her panties. She stares into my eyes the whole time. I love that she is so open. She's the kind of lover who is okay with the lights on or off. She even opens her stance a little bit to allow me to tease her slit through the slick fabric.

Her mouth is on mine the second she hangs up the phone. Our kiss is deep and slow until I slip my fingers into her panties. She's already swollen. I can't get to her fast enough.

"Let's go to my room." She breaks apart from me, her chest heaving. She grabs her pants off of the floor and we head back to her bedroom. She locks the door just in case an hour really means forty-five minutes.

It's different this time. She's more in tune with me. It feels right. She's watching me and touching me while I do the same to her. I can feel myself slip even further in love with her. It's not something I want to think about because I still don't know how to handle it. I want to show her how I feel. It's the safest way right now. I run my fingertips from her neck down to her hip. I kiss her mouth, her collarbone, the sensitive skin right above her breasts. Her featherlike touches burn me with need and I'm overcome with emotions.

I'm mortified when I feel tears slide down my cheeks. She stops me and pulls me close to her. I can't stop crying. So much for playing it cool and being able to walk away from this casual relationship. She wraps a blanket around us and holds me until I get control of myself. I don't even know what to tell her. What just happened? She kisses the top of my head and runs her hand up and down my arm. I've decided this is the best place to be, right here with her. I don't want to go to Italy and be apart for almost a year. I'll never survive.

"It's okay. You've had an emotional twenty-four hours. Totally understandable." She's trying to console me. I have no idea what to say to her. After about two minutes or ten, I'm finally able to talk.

"So much for the great seduction I had planned."

She squeezes me softly against her. "It's okay. We have time before you leave. But we don't have a lot of time now, unfortunately." I look at her clock. It's been forty minutes already.

"Did I fall asleep or something? How did we lose that much time?" I'm perplexed. She smiles at me and wipes away the last of my tears.

"Don't worry about it. Why don't you freshen up and I'll get started in the kitchen. I want my mum to see you as the happy scholarship recipient, not the sad woman who's had a very emotionally charged week." She leans up and kisses me softly. She kisses my wet cheeks and I can't help but hug her.

"Thank you," I say. She nods against me. I sniffle for a bit, grab my clothes and head for her bathroom. I lean over the sink and look at myself in the mirror. My eyes are puffy, and my cheeks and nose are red. My heart is raw. I splash water on my face until the heat of my emotions cools down and I'm no longer splotchy. I use her hairbrush and braid my hair back from my face. My shirt and shorts are wrinkled, but I have no choice but to put them on. I wet my hands and smooth out the wrinkles the best that I can and give myself a final look over. Better than I was, but not quite myself. My smile doesn't reach my eyes.

I take a deep breath and head into the kitchen. Evelyn and Olivia aren't here yet, so I have a few minutes alone with Taryn.

"You doing better?" She gives me another hug. I can feel the sting of tears in my eyes so I hug her back fiercely. I'm the first to break it.

"I'm really sorry about that. I don't know what happened," I say.

She waves it off. "No worries. It's been a crazy week for you. Quit worrying and quit apologizing. Let's make some pasta." She is able to get my mind off of my breakdown and we are making fresh pasta when her mother and Olivia arrive.

"Pie! You're here!" Olivia runs over for a hug. I squeeze her just a bit too tight and she squeaks. I quickly apologize to her and pull her braids playfully. "Grandma, this is Ki, but I call her pie. She calls me stinky."

"I've heard so much about you, Ki. It's nice to finally meet you," Evelyn says. She looks like Taryn, only shorter, but with the same grace and poise.

"It's nice to meet you, too." I'm nervous. I don't know if she knows about our personal relationship or just our professional one. "Have you enjoyed your stay so far?"

"I can't wait until we move back for good. I do miss the quick and easy things here in the United States."

"When do you think you'll move back for good?"

"In two years. We'll just have to figure out where Taryn and Olivia will put down roots. Even though I'm from the northeast, this city has quite the charm and the cost of living is palatable." I smile at her culinary reference.

"Why do I get the feeling Taryn isn't the only cook in your family?"

Evelyn laughs. "That girl taught us all how to cook. Not a skill she acquired from either of us." She has a slight accent, like Olivia, but not nearly as strong as Taryn's.

"Well, she's fantastic and I've learned so much from her. I hope she puts down roots here, too." Our conversation is light and fun, even Olivia hangs around to participate. She's very well behaved for a six-year-old.

Taryn and I start the pasta and put Olivia in charge of cranking the handle of the machine that will flatten the dough. I help her because she's not strong enough to do it on her own, but I pretend that she's doing it all herself. I catch Taryn watching us and my heart jumps and twirls. I think about what a life with her could be like. She's great at masking her emotions and only smiles at me when we make eye contact. Evelyn is very laid back and a great conversationalist. Her stories of living in South Africa are amazing, probably more so because I've never been out of the country. I would love to visit someday. Evelyn is sweet and extends an open invitation to visit until they move back to the United States for good.

When it's time to stack the lasagna into the pan, Olivia wants to help, but the noodles and the sauce are both too hot for her to handle so I give her the job of sprinkling the cheese on the sauce between the layers. Evelyn watches us, openly, without judgment.

"Grandma, let's go to the pool," Olivia says.

"Wait, you don't want to help us clean up?" I ask.

Olivia rolls her eyes at me. "That's the worst part." I agree.

"When will dinner be ready?" Evelyn asks.

"We can cook it whenever. Just plan for dinner at six." It's four now.

"Are you staying, Ki?" Olivia asks.

"I helped make it. Of course I'm staying." I roll my eyes back at her. She giggles.

"Go put your swimsuit on," Taryn says. "Mum, are you going to be okay in the heat?" Evelyn waves her off.

"It's not that hot out. I'll wear my hat. I might even get into the pool, too." She disappears to change, too, and it's just me and Taryn in the kitchen.

"I like your mom a lot."

Taryn smiles. "She likes you, too. She normally isn't this chatty," she says. Clean up doesn't take us long and we finish stacking the dishwasher just as Evelyn and Olivia head out the door.

"Have fun, ladies," I say.

"Why don't you come with us, Ki?" Olivia asks. She's hopeful and it actually hurts me to have to say no.

"Maybe later we can go. Go spend time with Grandma." She nods her head and follows Evelyn out the door. I turn to Taryn.

"It's amazing how thoughtful Olivia is. She genuinely thinks about suggestions before making a decision. She did that in the River Plaza the first time I met her. That's so remarkable for her age," I say.

"I try to give her the opportunity to think things through before she makes a decision."

"Most parents don't have the patience to do that."

Taryn fixes us iced tea and we sit on the couch. I'm nervous because the last time we were alone I had a meltdown. I'm drained so I don't think that will happen again. She holds my hand and I smile at the warm gesture.

"So what are your plans between now and when you have to leave?" she asks.

"I really haven't given it much thought. I can sublet the apartment and Jessie has already promised to take care of Sophia. Past that, I have no idea."

"I can't believe I'm saying this, but we can take care of Sophia, too."

I look at her, my eyes wide with surprise. "That's a great idea. Then Olivia can play with a cat and figure out if she's going to like having one around. You would want to watch my cat while I'm gone?" This is big. This is relationship talk, not casual talk.

"Sophia loves me. Of course I would watch her. I mean, I'm sure she's closer to Jessie having known her for years, but Olivia would be thrilled and would play with her every day."

"Okay, if you're sure, I would love that and so would Sophia." I'm shocked that she wants to do this. She barely knows Sophia. Plus, I think that with Olivia chasing her most of the day, Sophia might even bring out her kitten side and play more. I'm a bad mom. I'm okay with her getting virtually zero exercise and hanging out with me on the couch. "Do you even like cats?" She laughs.

"I like all animals. Sophia is sweet and she loves me. I can't imagine it being a bad idea." Wait until it storms. She might rethink that.

"Now that school is done, you can bring Olivia over one day so she can meet her and we can make it a done deal," I say. Taryn nods. I notice I'm sliding down the couch more, exhaustion settling in. Taryn reaches for a pillow.

"Here, put your head down on my lap." She taps the pillow with her hand. I sprawl out and put my head down. She plays with my hair and within a minute, I'm asleep. I don't even feel her leave to put the lasagna in the oven or take it out. I wake up to a tiny finger touching my face. At first, I think I'm home and Sophia is nudging me to feed her, but the poke doesn't feel furry. I feel it on my cheek, then my nose, then my eyebrow. I realize it's Olivia by her feeble attempt at stifling a giggle. When her finger gets close to my mouth I pretend to bite it and she screams.

"Olivia!" Taryn says, but I raise my hand to let Taryn know I'm awake. I reach out to grab Olivia, but she scoots out of the way. I growl and she runs into the kitchen to hide behind Taryn. I sit up and see Evelyn watching me. I blush because I completely forgot she was in town. I'm embarrassed.

"That was a much needed nap. I'm sorry." I don't know why I've apologized to her, but it feels like the right thing to do.

"Don't apologize, dear. Long week for you, I'm sure," she says.

I look over at Taryn and notice she finished cooking and prepping everything for our meal. "Why didn't you wake me?" I walk into the kitchen to see if there is something I can do.

Taryn smiles at me. "I tried to but you grumbled at me."

"Did I really? I'm sorry."

"Don't worry. It was cute. You can help me with the drinks. What do you want to drink? I have a nice Cabernet Sauvignon or we have tea or ice water."

"I'll open the wine if you or Evelyn would like a glass. I'm going to stick with water. I think I'm dehydrated." She hands me the bottle and opener and I open it like an expert, impressing even myself.

"I want a glass," Olivia says.

"No, you don't. You want a juice box or milk or water like me," I say.

"I told you. Six going on sixteen," Taryn says. She rolls her eyes at Olivia and Olivia laughs.

"Okay, I'll have water like Ki," she says. I help her with the ice and we put our water in wineglasses. She gets a kick out of it and then I realize I've given very thin glass to a six-year-old.

"Be careful and don't drop the glass or clink it against anything too hard, okay?" She nods and carefully carries her glass over to the table with both hands. I take Taryn and Evelyn's glasses over to the table in case Olivia spills them.

"You are very good with children, Ki," Evelyn says.

"Thank you. I'm rarely around them though. They are fun little people." Olivia high fives me and we all laugh. We start dinner and have a great time talking, eating, sharing, and just being women. It's very peaceful and I find myself enjoying the night more so than last night with Jessie. I need roots. I need love. I need this. It's eight before we even think to get up and start cleaning the table off. Taryn shuffles Olivia off to get ready for bed. She asks that we all tuck her in. I tell her that if she hurries up, we will all read her a quick story. She runs off and Taryn and I work quickly to clean up the kitchen. We aren't quite done by the time Olivia is in bed so Evelyn goes to Olivia's bedroom to help pick out a book so that we can finish. Taryn grabs me when Evelyn leaves and pulls me close to her. She puts her forehead against mine and kisses my nose.

"You're great with my family. Thank you," she says.

I lean up and kiss her lips. "Your family is wonderful and I enjoy them. No need to thank me." I kiss her again, but break apart when it starts getting heavy. Now is definitely not the time. I point down the hall and give her a look and she laughs at me.

"You're right. Let's hurry up and get back there to them." We are done within five minutes and head back to Olivia's room.

"We picked out a story already." Olivia is fully awake, her eyes shining with excitement. She's holding a thin board book that looks like she's had it a few years. *"Giraffes Can't Dance* is my favorite book." I know her reading capabilities are higher, but it looks like a quick read and I don't argue.

"We can have some fun and each of us reads one word in order instead of just one reading," I say. We hunch over the book and read it that way until we are all laughing too hard to finish. I end up speed reading the book out loud so that we can leave and Olivia can go to sleep. She laughs the entire time. Evelyn and I say good night to her while Taryn tucks her in. Taryn's back in a few minutes.

"Out like a light." She sits next to me on the couch. I almost have another meltdown when she holds my hand. My heart races and throbs inside of my body because her mother is watching our entire exchange. I'm playing it cool. I haven't been around any of my girlfriends' parents mainly because I didn't care before. Evelyn seems unaffected by it and I eventually relax. When ten rolls around, Evelyn decides to retire for the night. I automatically stand when she does and she smiles at me.

"It has been a pleasure meeting you, Ki. I hope I get to see you again before I leave," she says. She hugs me and again I'm plagued by tears. What is wrong with me? I manage to keep them inside, but I know my eyes are glassy. She kisses Taryn and disappears down the hall. I can't pretend I'm not close to tears.

"I have no idea why I'm still emotional." I plop down next to Taryn and she puts her arm around me. I rest my head on her shoulder.

"You need plenty of rest, not just a cat nap here and there. Please sleep tonight," she says.

We sit on the couch and talk and kiss quietly and softly for the next two hours. It's midnight before I untangle myself and head home. Thankfully, I live only a few minutes away from her apartment so the drive isn't bad. I spend the time in my car trying to figure out my life. What is the most important thing to me? I'm still questioning everything by the time I crawl into bed.

❖

I wake up after almost ten hours of sleep and have an incredible urge to go to the market. Shopping with Taryn yesterday got me in the groove and I'm excited to find something new to cook. I shower, throw my hair back into a messy bun, and hit the ground running. I know I'm too late for the great stuff, but there are still enough good vegetables to pick through. I reach the end of the last aisle and see Mary walking into her new soon to be café. I follow her and knock on the door. She motions for me to come in.

"What do you think, Ki?"

"I love it. It's so much bigger than it looks." I look around and see so much potential. "I'm so proud of you. When do you think you will have this up and running?"

"Well, we're still working things out with the bank. I have the key from the realtor and technically, I shouldn't be in here, but I'm too excited to just wait around for the money. Oh my, God. I forgot to congratulate you on the scholarship. I'm so happy for you." She is genuine. I tell her Taryn said she came in second during the meal and she laughs with delight. "I'm so happy I beat him at something. Too bad you're leaving though. I'm going to miss you." She shows me around the place and I'm impressed with the ovens and kitchen space. The menu she has planned is very sweet and I encourage her to branch out and cook quiches and stuffed pastries with egg, sausage, and cheese. She looks at me like I'm crazy. "I bake. I'm a baker. The other stuff scares me."

"Maybe when you get comfortable you'll branch out more." I gather up my bags and wait for her to lock up. "I'm so excited for you. Do you have a name yet?"

"Not yet. I'm still thinking about it. I don't want it to be Mary's Something. My parents are pushing for my name to be in it, but sometimes that's not the best idea. Hopefully, I will think of it before we sign the papers." I wish her luck and head home. I'm so jealous of Mary. Yes, I'm going to cook at a world famous cooking school, but Mary is living her dream.

CHAPTER TWENTY-SEVEN

I can't believe I'm doing this. I don't know if I'm scared or excited or one step away from a major panic attack. My knee bounces frantically up and down. I wipe my palms on my pants for the fifth time. I hate waiting.

"I'm sorry, Ki. He said he would be here soon. Can I get you anything to drink?" Linda, Dr. Wright's assistant, has always been very nice to the students. Why she works for that asshat, I'll never know. Maybe she balances out his evilness.

"I'm fine, Linda. Thank you." I'm thinking of heading to one of the kitchens to fix lunch because I wasn't hungry when I got here two hours ago, but I am now. I thumb through the same magazine that has been resting in my lap. This time, I play the game where I pick one thing on each page that I can't live without. My sister and I used to do that with the large department store catalogs that my grandmother had out on her coffee table.

"Ki, I'm sorry I've kept you waiting so long." Dr. Wright enters the office all smiles. I see a ketchup stain on his tie and I can't help myself. Besides, I've graduated.

"I trust lunch was yummy." I point to his tie and he has the decency to blush.

"Yes, and it ran late. Come into my office," he says. I follow him inside and make myself comfortable on the couch. He has a stack of papers in the guest chair and there isn't anywhere else to sit. "I have several forms for you to fill out. Are you ready for your trip to Italy?"

"Well, that's what I want to talk about. I worked hard to get that scholarship and beat out all of my classmates. I'm honored to have it, but I want to turn it down and give it to Scott McDonnell." Dr. Wright's eyes bug out.

"You want to give up your scholarship?" I nod. "Do you know how hard other students worked to try to get this opportunity and you just want to throw it away?" He's starting to upset me.

"First of all, I didn't take it away from anybody. I earned it. You know that better than anybody else. I worked hard and won it fair and square. I didn't resort to cheating like Scott did." I hold up my hand to stop him when he actually tries to defend him. "He's an ass and should have been kicked out for what he did, but you had your reasons for keeping him. Just don't try to convince me. We both know the truth." I don't know where my tenacity is coming from, but I'm going with it. "A bigger and better opportunity has come up for me and I plan on taking advantage of it. It's why I went to culinary school in the first place. If I default on the scholarship, is it transferrable to the runner-up?"

"I believe it is. I just hope Mr. McDonnell can accept it days after the fact," he says. I look at him like he's crazy.

"We both know he's at his parents' restaurant prepping stew or something. I'm sure he will jump at the opportunity." We stare at each other until it becomes uncomfortable. "Well, I guess that's all I have. Thank you for understanding." Like he had a choice. I stand and he surprises me by shaking my hand.

"You've been a great student, Ki. It's been a pleasure watching you grow into an amazing chef. I look forward to hearing about you in the culinary world." I thank him and leave his office.

I feel lighter with every step that takes me away from Kirkwood Academy. The entire experience was great, but the last semester really changed me, as a chef and as a woman. Taryn pushed us all to improve on what we knew and taught us how to focus under pressure. It was the perfect ending to a long journey.

CHAPTER TWENTY-EIGHT

"K i! Where are you?" I hear my front door open and peek out of my bedroom to see Taryn standing in the hallway looking for me. She does not look happy. I really should lock my front door.

"I'm back here. I'll be right out." I need to find a T-shirt. I'm sure she just found out I turned down the scholarship. Apparently, she isn't as happy about it as I am. She's in my room within a few seconds, her face flushed.

"What did you do?" she asks.

I hold my shirt up to my chest, covering myself from her and her anger. "Hi, Taryn. Come in. Would you like something to drink?"

"Don't play with me, Ki. Why did you turn down the scholarship? That was everything to you. How could you just walk away from such a fantastic opportunity?" I wasn't expecting her to jump into my arms and confess her undying love for me, but I certainly didn't think she would be this upset.

"A better opportunity came up."

"What are you talking about?" she asks. I slip on my shirt and walk over to her. Everything about her body language tells me to tread lightly.

"I need to show you something. Will you take a ride with me?"

"Only if you tell me what the hell is going on."

"How about you come with me and then I'll tell you what the hell is going on." I'm starting to get pissed. She's scolding me like a child. She unclenches her fists and her shoulders slump.

"I just hope you have a really good explanation."

"I understand your concern, but I think you can trust me by now," I say. She nods then reaches out to me. I walk into her hug. She holds me and kisses my head.

"I do trust you."

I pull away and stare at her. "Then let me finish getting dressed and I'll show you what I'm talking about." She sits on the bed and patiently waits for me to slip into my shorts and find my sandals. I walk over to her and kiss her softly. "Let's go."

"What are we doing here?" she asks as we approach the River Plaza.

"It will all make sense in a few minutes." My heart is pumping and I can hear it throb in my ears. We walk past all of the aisles until we hit the row of restaurants at the far end, near downtown. I point to Mary's cafe. "See that? Mary and I are opening up a café down here. I gave up the scholarship because my dream is to have my own restaurant. Yes, Italy would be great, but this is really what I want." She walks up to the storefront and looks inside. "Do you want to go in? I have a key."

"I can't believe you did this. This is fantastic. Let's go inside." I'm giddy as I unlock the door. I think she's even more excited than I am. "Whose idea was this?" Her smile is sincere and I know I made the right decision.

"Mary was going to have her parents as partners and open a bakery, but I thought it might be nice if the bakery was actually a café and we offered more than just sweets. We're still working out the menu, but we'll have different types of quiche, panini, and other non-sweet items. We're thinking six in the morning until two in the afternoon. Hopefully, we can hire people to help, but for now it will just be us and maybe her little sister if we need a cashier."

Taryn wraps her arms around me and squeezes me. "I'm so proud of you. This is absolutely perfect. And I'm proud of Mary, too, for really going for it. Honestly, I didn't think she had it in her."

"It was a surprise to me, too, but Mary has her act together. She knew at the beginning of the semester that she didn't have much of a chance to win the scholarship so she went looking for her dream and found it."

"Ki, not to be nosy, but how can you afford this?"

"Well, culinary school is expensive, but not as expensive as law school. The rest of my trust fund covered the costs and we'll get a business loan for supplies. We won't have a lot of debt. Hopefully, we can pay it off quickly. We just need to get the word out when we open the café."

"Oh, I'm sure the institute would promote it. Two scholarship contenders join forces to open a restaurant right after graduation. It's brilliant," she says. I don't think I've ever seen her this genuinely happy before. I can't help but beam with her.

"You think so? That would be great for business right away. I'm sure J.D. is crushing on me after my chicken mole blew his mind. He might even make it mandatory for his students to go."

Taryn laughs. "J.D. isn't the only one crushing on you."

"Who else? Scott? Nah. Thankfully, he will be gone." She slips her arms around my waist. "Maybe Mr. Stewart. He's always looked at me appreciatively." Taryn squeezes my waist.

"Oh, really?" She lifts her eyebrow at me.

"And then there's Mary." I'm rewarded with a tickling that has me squealing. She stops the torture, and pulls me closer to her, my T-shirt crumpled in her fists.

"There better not be Mary." Her voice is a playful growl. "At least not that way. You're mine." We both stop and stare at one another. I'm no longer giggling.

"I'm yours, huh?" I say. My voice sounds quiet and low.

"I don't know what you want, but I know I would like to continue our relationship. I enjoy our time together and now we won't have to hide when we are out in public." Do I want this? Is she crazy? How could she not know that I am head over heels for her.

"Maybe we could still keep this up." I try to be uninterested, but my heart is tumbling inside my chest, anxious to latch onto any words of encouragement. I realize she is dead serious so I sober up quickly. I lean up and kiss her lips. "I definitely want to keep this up. I think you are a beautiful woman inside and out and I can't wait to cook with you, and spend weekends together, and go to movies, and hold hands, and go for long walks, and do all the things that people who are together do." I don't want to call her a girlfriend yet, but hopefully she knows that I'm committed to her and only her. I decide to clarify quickly. "It's only you. No one else." She rewards me with a slow, meaningful kiss. I sigh against her.

"As unbelievably selfish as this sounds, I'm glad you aren't leaving," she says.

"I am, too." We spend a good thirty minutes inside the café looking at the place, studying the ovens and layout of the small dining area. There's probably room for six round tables and a small bar area that will either be a place for self-serving coffee or chairs for additional seating. "Mary is going to have so many different types of cheesecakes, pastries and muffins. People will be able to order in advance. The ovens can handle several cakes and pies at once so hopefully we can keep up."

"Have you told anybody about this yet?" she asks.

Holy Christ, I forgot to tell my mom! She still thinks I'm going to Italy. That conversation is going to be another heartbreaker for her. I set a mental reminder to visit her tomorrow before word gets out and she hears it from somebody else.

"Not really. I mentioned to Jessie that I had an idea, but she doesn't know that I actually went through with it. I really wanted to tell you first since you have been an inspiration to me and have been incredibly supportive." I'm embarrassed that I'm sappy and completely surprised when I see Taryn wipe away a tear. I've never seen her crack before. "I can't imagine leaving you and Olivia now. Don't you see how perfect this is? I get the girl and the dream job. I know this is probably too soon, but Taryn, I love you." Great, now I'm starting to cry. She's crying even harder. We're a complete mess. "Do you remember when we were on our bike ride? That was the exact moment I realized I loved you. I've never been in love before and I had a panic attack because my feelings were so strong and I didn't know how to get them out." Taryn is clutching me, not saying a word. Now she's starting to scare me. "Please tell me you feel the same way. Tell me that I didn't just make a complete ass of myself." She laughs before she looks at me.

"Ki, I love you, too. So very much. I wanted to tell you that weekend, too, but I thought that it would be selfish for me to say it. I want you to have the Italian cooking school experience, but I'm so much happier with this choice." She kisses me soundly, passionately, telling me everything I need to feel in that one kiss. It leaves me breathless.

"Say it again."

"I love you." She pulls me close again. I start shaking in her arms.

"I'll never get tired of hearing that from you or saying it to you."

She presses her forehead against mine. "I know."

EPILOGUE

C an you believe the turnout?" Mary asks. We look at one another. I'm trying not to be overwhelmed right now, but it's hard when there's about twenty people inside the café and another thirty waiting to come in. So much for standing back and being the renowned chefs. We dive in to help Mary's sister and cousin take orders, fill orders, and give change. I look up and see Taryn and Olivia in the doorway. I wink at her and motion for her to come in the back.

"Hi, babe. I'd ask how it's going, but I can see it's going well." She kisses my cheek and Olivia gives me a quick hug. It's been two months since we've confessed our love and I feel invincible. Our relationship is perfect. My lease on my apartment is up in a month and Taryn asked me to move in with them until we can find a place together. "I have a feeling it's going to be busier this weekend. Dr. Wright told the entire academy to visit and see what two successful chefs can do with certificates from Kirkwood." I roll my eyes and she laughs. "Hey, free press is good press."

I nod. "Free tastes help, too." I point outside where Mary's parents have set up tables with samples for the patrons of the River Plaza. My mom is here, too, bragging more than helping, but bringing us business. When she found out I turned down the scholarship, she was surprisingly supportive. I don't think she wanted me gone that long. When she found out it was to open a café she cried, but this time tears of joy. She might even be happier than if I got my law degree. At least now she can bring her friends here and boast about her daughter having her own café.

"And they're delicious. Right, Olivia?" Taryn asks.

"I love the strawberry rolls," she says.

"You didn't try the quiche?" Olivia wrinkles her nose up at me. "Well, one day you'll love quiche." She shakes her head at me. I roll my eyes at her. She laughs.

"I'm proud of you, love. The place looks great. Ideal location, perfect family environment. You'll do well here. And the sign looks great," Taryn says.

"I'm glad we finally came up with a name. It was easier than we thought it would be." The name of our pride and joy, our dream come true sits in red porcelain letters above the door: Taste.

About the Author

Kris Bryant grew up a military brat living in several different countries before her family settled down in the Midwest when she was twelve. Books were her only form of entertainment overseas, and she read anything and everything within her reach. Reading eventually turned into writing when she decided she didn't like the way some of the novels ended and wanted to give the characters she fell in love with the ending she thought they so deserved.

Earning a B.A. in English from the University of Missouri, Kris focused more on poetry, and after some encouragement from her girlfriend, decided to tackle her own book.

Kris can be contacted at krisbryantbooks@gmail.com

Website: http://www.krisbryant.net

Books Available from Bold Strokes Books

Camp Rewind by Meghan O'Brien. A summer camp for grown-ups becomes the site of an unlikely romance between a shy, introverted divorcee and one of the Internet's most infamous cultural critics—who attends undercover. (978-1-62639-793-4)

Cross Purposes by Gina L. Dartt. In pursuit of a lost Acadian treasure, three women must not only work out the clues, but also the complicated tangle of emotion and attraction developing between them. (978-1-62639-713-2)

Imperfect Truth by C.A. Popovich. Can an imperfect truth stand in the way of love? (978-1-62639-787-3)

Life in Death by M. Ullrich. Sometimes the devastating end is your only chance for a new beginning. (978-1-62639-773-6)

Love on Liberty by MJ Williamz. Hearts collide when politics clash. (978-1-62639-639-5)

Serious Potential by Maggie Cummings. Pro golfer Tracy Allen plans to forget her ex during a visit to Bay West, a lesbian condo community in NYC, but when she meets Dr. Jennifer Betsy, she gets more than she bargained for. (978-1-62639-633-3)

Taste by Kris Bryant. Accomplished chef Taryn has walked away from her promising career in the city's top restaurant to devote her life to her five-year-old daughter and is content until Ki Blake comes along. (978-1-62639-718-7)

The Second Wave by Jean Copeland. Can star-crossed lovers have a second chance after decades apart, or does the love of a lifetime only happen once? (978-1-62639-830-6)

Valley of Fire by Missouri Vaun. Taken captive in a desert outpost after their small aircraft is hijacked, Ava and her captivating passenger discover things about each other and themselves that will change them both forever. (978-1-62639-496-4)

Basic Training of the Heart by Jaycie Morrison. In 1944, socialite Elizabeth Carlton joins the Women's Army Corps to escape family expectations and love's disappointments. Can Sergeant Gale Rains get her through Basic Training with their hearts intact? (978-1-62639-818-4)

Before by KE Payne. When Tally falls in love with her band's new recruit, she has a tough decision to make. What does she want more—Alex or the band? (978-1-62639-677-7)

Believing in Blue by Maggie Morton. Growing up gay in a small town has been hard, but it can't compare to the next challenge Wren—with her new, sky-blue wings—faces: saving two entire worlds. (978-1-62639-691-3)

Coils by Barbara Ann Wright. A modern young woman follows her aunt into the Greek Underworld and makes a pact with Medusa to win her freedom by killing a hero of legend. (978-1-62639-598-5)

Courting the Countess by Jenny Frame. When relationship-phobic Lady Henrietta Knight starts to care about housekeeper Annie Brannigan and her daughter, can she overcome her fears and promise Annie the forever that she demands? (978-1-62639-785-9)

Dapper by Jenny Frame. Amelia Honey meets the mysterious Byron De Brek and is faced with her darkest fantasies, but will her strict moral upbringing stop her from exploring what she truly wants? (978-1-62639-898-6E)

Delayed Gratification: The Honeymoon by Meghan O'Brien. A dream European honeymoon turns into a winter storm nightmare involving a delayed flight, a ditched rental car, and eventually, a surprisingly happy ending. (978-1-62639-766-8E)

For Money or Love by Heather Blackmore. Jessica Spaulding must choose between ignoring the truth to keep everything she has, and doing the right thing only to lose it all—including the woman she loves. (978-1-62639-756-9)

Hooked by Jaime Maddox. With the help of sexy Detective Mac Calabrese, Dr. Jessica Benson is working hard to overcome her past, but it may not be enough to stop a murderer. (978-1-62639-689-0)

Lands End by Jackie D. Public relations superstar Amy Kline is dealing with a media nightmare, and the last thing she expects is for restaurateur Lena Michaels to change everything, but she will. (978-1-62639-739-2)

Lysistrata Cove by Dena Hankins. Jack and Eve navigate the maelstrom of their darkest desires and find love by transgressing gender, dominance, submission, and the law on the crystal blue Caribbean Sea. (978-1-62639-821-4)

Twisted Screams by Sheri Lewis Wohl. Reluctant psychic Lorna Dutton doesn't want to forgive, but if she doesn't do just that an innocent woman will die. (978-1-62639-647-0)

A Class Act by Tammy Hayes. Buttoned-up college professor Dr. Margaret Parks doesn't know what she's getting herself into when she agrees to one date with her student, Rory Morgan, who is 15 years her junior. (978-1-62639-701-9)

Bitter Root by Laydin Michaels. Small town chef Adi Bergeron is hiding something, and Griffith McNaulty is going to find out what it is even if it gets her killed. (978-1-62639-656-2)

Capturing Forever by Erin Dutton. When family pulls Jacqueline and Casey back together, will the lessons learned in eight years apart be enough to mend the mistakes of the past? (978-1-62639-631-9)

Deception by VK Powell. DEA Agent Colby Vincent and Attorney Adena Weber are embroiled in a drug investigation involving homeless veterans and an attraction that could destroy them both. (978-1-62639-596-1)

Dyre: A Knight of Spirit and Shadows by Rachel E. Bailey. With the abduction of her queen, werewolf-bodyguard Des must follow the kidnappers' trail to Europe, where her queen—and a battle unlike any Des has ever waged—awaits her. (978-1-62639-664-7)

First Position by Melissa Brayden. Love and rivalry take center stage for Anastasia Mikhelson and Natalie Frederico in one of the most prestigious ballet companies in the nation. (978-1-62639-602-9)

Best Laid Plans by Jan Gayle. Nicky and Lauren are meant for each other, but Nicky's haunting past and Lauren's societal fears threaten to derail all possibilities of a relationship. (987-1-62639-658-6)

Exchange by CF Frizzell. When Shay Maguire rode into rural Montana, she never expected to meet the woman of her dreams—or to learn Mel Baker was held hostage by legal agreement to her right-wing father. (987-1-62639-679-1)

Just Enough Light by AJ Quinn. Will a serial killer's return to Colorado destroy Kellen Ryan and Dana Kingston's chance at love, or can the search-and-rescue team save themselves? (987-1-62639-685-2)

Rise of the Rain Queen by Fiona Zedde. Nyandoro is nobody's princess. She fights, curses, fornicates, and gets into as much trouble as her brothers. But the path to a throne is not always the one we expect. (987-1-62639-592-3)

Tales from Sea Glass Inn by Karis Walsh. Over the course of a year at Cannon Beach, tourists and locals alike find solace and passion at the Sea Glass Inn. (987-1-62639-643-2)

The Color of Love by Radclyffe. Black sheep Derian Winfield needs to convince literary agent Emily May to marry her to save the Winfield Agency and solve Emily's green card problem, but Derian didn't count on falling in love. (987-1-62639-716-3)

A Reluctant Enterprise by Gun Brooke. When two women grow up learning nothing but distrust, unworthiness, and abandonment, it's no wonder they are apprehensive and fearful when an overwhelming love just won't be denied. (978-1-62639-500-8)

†

Above the Law by Carsen Taite. Love is the last thing on Agent Dale Nelson's mind, but reporter Lindsey Ryan's investigation could change the way she sees everything—her career, her past, and her future. (978-1-62639-558-9)

Jane's World: The Case of the Mail Order Bride by Paige Braddock. Jane's PayBuddy account gets hacked and she inadvertently purchases a mail order bride from the Eastern Bloc. (978-1-62639-494-0)

Love's Redemption by Donna K. Ford. For ex-convict Rhea Daniels and ex-priest Morgan Scott, redemption lies in the thin line between right and wrong. (978-1-62639-673-9)

The Shewstone by Jane Fletcher. The prophetic Shewstone is in Eawynn's care, but unfortunately for her, Matt is coming to steal it. (978-1-62639-554-1)

Milton Keynes UK
Ingram Content Group UK Ltd.
UKHW041318210923
429119UK00001B/83